John Brown, John Cairns

Supplementary chapter to the life of Rev. John Brown, D.D

A letter to Rev. John Cairns, D.D

John Brown, John Cairns

Supplementary chapter to the life of Rev. John Brown, D.D
A letter to Rev. John Cairns, D.D

ISBN/EAN: 9783337108342

Printed in Europe, USA, Canada, Australia, Japan

Cover: Foto ©Andreas Hilbeck / pixelio.de

More available books at **www.hansebooks.com**

MEMOIR OF JOHN BROWN, D.D.

LETTER TO REV. DR. CAIRNS,

BY JOHN BROWN, M.D.

LETTER.*

23 Rutland Street, 15th *August*.

My dear Friend,—When, at the urgent request of his trustees and family, and in accordance with what I believe was his own wish, you undertook my father's Memoir, it was in a measure on the understanding that I would furnish you with some domestic and personal details. This I hoped to have done, but was unable.

Though convinced more than ever how little my hand is needed, I will now endeavour to fulfil my promise. Before doing so, however, you must permit me to express our deep gratitude to you for this crowning proof of your regard for him

"Without whose life we had not been;"

to whom for many years you habitually wrote as "My father," and one of whose best blessings, when he was "such an one as Paul the aged," was to know that you were to him "mine own son in the gospel."

With regard to the manner in which you

* To the Rev. John Cairns, D.D., Berwick-on-Tweed.

2 D

have done this last kindness to the dead, I can say nothing more expressive of our feelings, and, I am sure, nothing more gratifying to you, than that the record you have given of my father's life, and of the series of great public questions in which he took part, is done in the way which would have been most pleasing to himself—that which, with his passionate love of truth and liberty, his relish for concentrated, just thought and expression, and his love of being loved, he would have most desired, in any one speaking of him after he was gone. He would, I doubt not, say, as one said to a great painter, on looking at his portrait, "It is certainly like, but it is much better looking;" and you might well reply as did the painter, "It is the truth, told lovingly"—and all the more true that it is so told. You have, indeed, been enabled to speak the truth, or as the Greek has it, ἀληθεύειν ἐν ἀγάπῃ—to truth it in love.

I have over and over again sat down to try and do what I promised and wished—to give some faint expression of my father's life; not of what he did or said or wrote—not even of what he was as a man of God and a public teacher; but what he was in his essential nature—what he would have been had he been anything else than what he was, or had lived a thousand years ago.

Sometimes I have this so vividly in my mind that I think I have only to sit down and write it off, and do it to the quick. "The idea of his life," what he was as a whole, what was his self, all his days, would,—to go on with words which not time or custom can ever wither or make stale,—

> "Sweetly creep
> Into my study of imagination;
> And every lovely organ of his life
> Would come apparelled in more precious habit—
> More moving delicate, and full of life,
> Into the eye and prospect of my soul,
> Than when he lived indeed,"

as if the sacredness of death and the bloom of eternity were on it; or as you may have seen in an untroubled lake, the heaven reflected with its clouds, brighter, purer, more exquisite than itself; but when you try to put this into words, to detain yourself over it, it is by this very act disturbed, broken and bedimmed, and soon vanishes away, as would the imaged heavens in the lake, if a pebble were cast into it, or a breath of wind stirred its face. The very anxiety to transfer it, as it looked out of the clear darkness of the past, makes the image grow dim and disappear.

Every one whose thoughts are not seldom

with the dead, must have felt both these conditions; how, in certain passive, tranquil states, there comes up into the darkened chamber of the mind, its "chamber of imagery"—uncalled, as if it blossomed out of space, exact, absolute, consummate, vivid, speaking, not darkly as in a glass, but face to face, and "moving delicate"—this "idea of his life;" and then how an effort to prolong and perpetuate and record all this, troubles the vision and kills it!   It is as if one should try to paint in a mirror the reflection of a dear and unseen face; the coarse, uncertain, passionate handling and colour, ineffectual and hopeless, shut out the very thing itself.

I will therefore give this up as in vain, and try by some fragmentary sketches, scenes, and anecdotes, to let you know in some measure what manner of man my father was. Anecdotes, if true and alive, are always valuable; the man in the concrete, the *totus quis* comes out in them; and I know you too well to think that you will consider as trivial or out of place anything in which his real nature displayed itself, and your own sense of humour as a master and central power of the human soul, playing about the very essence of the man, will do more than forgive anything of this kind which may crop out here and there, like the smile of wild-flowers in grass, or by the wayside.

My first recollection of my father, my first impression, not only of his character, but of his eyes and face and presence, strange as it may seem, dates from my fifth year. Doubtless I had looked at him often enough before that, and had my own childish thoughts about him ; but this was the time when I got my fixed, compact idea of him, and the first look of him which I felt could never be forgotten. I saw him, as it were, by a flash of lightning, sudden and complete. A child begins by seeing bits of everything ; it knows in part—here a little, there a little ; it makes up its wholes out of its own littles, and is long of reaching the fulness of a whole ; and in this we are children all our lives in much. Children are long of seeing, or at least of looking at what is above them ; they like the ground, and its flowers and stones, its " red sodgers " and lady-birds, and all its queer things ; their world is about three feet high, and they are more often stooping than gazing up. I know I was past ten before I saw, or cared to see, the ceilings of the rooms in the manse at Biggar.

On the morning of the 28th May 1816, my eldest sister Janet and I were sleeping in the

kitchen-bed with Tibbie Meek,* our only servant.   We were all three awakened by a cry of
pain—sharp, insufferable, as if one were stung.
Years after we two confided to each other, sitting by the burnside, that we thought that
" great cry " which arose at midnight in Egypt
must have been like it.   We all knew whose
voice it was, and, in our night-clothes, we ran
into the passage, and into the little parlour
to the left hand, in which was a closet-bed.
We found my father standing before us, erect,
his hands clenched in his black hair, his eyes
full of misery and amazement, his face white as
that of the dead.   He frightened us.   He saw
this, or else his intense will had mastered his
agony, for, taking his hands from his head, he
said, slowly and gently, " Let us give thanks,"
and turned to a little sofa† in the room ; there
lay our mother, dead.   She had long been ailing.

* A year ago, I found an elderly country woman, a widow, waiting
for me. Rising up, she said, "D'ye mind me ?" I looked at her,
but could get nothing from her face ; but the voice remained in my
ear, as if coming from " the fields of sleep," and I said by a sort of
instinct, " Tibbie Meek ! " I had not seen her or heard her voice
for more than forty years. She had come to get some medical advice.
Voices are often like the smells of flowers and leaves, the tastes of
wild fruits—they touch and awaken memory in a strange way.
" Tibbie " is now living at Thankerton.

† This sofa, which was henceforward sacred in the house, he had
always beside him. He used to tell us he set her down upon it
when he brought her home to the manse.

I remember her sitting in a shawl,—an Indian one with little dark green spots on a light ground,—and watching her growing pale with what I afterwards knew must have been strong pain. She had, being feverish, slipped out of bed, and "grandmother," her mother, seeing her "change come," had called my father, and they two saw her open her blue, kind, and true eyes, "comfortable" to us all "as the day"—I remember them better than those of any one I saw yesterday—and, with one faint look of recognition to him, close them till the time of the restitution of all things.

"She had another morn than ours."

Then were seen in full action his keen, passionate nature, his sense of mental pain, and his supreme will, instant and unsparing, making himself and his terrified household give thanks in the midst of such a desolation,—and for it. Her warfare was accomplished, her iniquities were pardoned; she had already received from her Lord's hand double for all her sins : this was his supreme and over-mastering thought, and he gave it utterance.

No man was happier in his wives. My mother was modest, calm, thrifty, reasonable, tender, happy-hearted. She was his student-love, and is even now remembered in that pastoral region, for " her sweet gentleness and wife-like government." Her death and his sorrow and loss, settled down deep into the heart of the countryside. He was so young and bright, so full of fire, so unlike any one else, so devoted to his work, so chivalrous in his look and manner, so fearless, and yet so sensitive and self-contained. She was so wise, good and gentle, gracious and frank.

His subtlety of affection, and his almost cruel self-command, were shown on the day of the funeral. It was to Symington, four miles off,—a quiet little churchyard, lying in the shadow of Tinto ; a place where she herself had wished to be laid. The funeral was chiefly on horseback. We, the family, were in coaches. I had been since the death in a sort of stupid musing and wonder, not making out what it all meant. I knew my mother was said to be dead. I saw she was still, and laid out, and then shut up, and didn't move ; but I did not know that when she was carried out in that long black box, and we all went with her, she alone was never to return.

When we got to the village all the people were at their doors. One woman, the blacksmith Thomas Spence's wife, had a nursing baby in her arms, and he leapt up and crowed with joy at the strange sight, the crowding horsemen, the coaches and the nodding plumes of the hearse.   This was my brother William, then nine months old, and Margaret Spence was his foster-mother.   Those with me were overcome at this sight ; he of all in the world whose, in some ways, was the greatest loss, the least conscious, turning it to his own childish glee.

We got to the churchyard and stood round the open grave.   My dear old grandfather was asked by my father to pray ; he did.   I don't remember his words ; I believe he, through his tears and sobs, repeated the Divine words, "All flesh is grass, and all the glory of man as the flower of the grass ; the grass withereth, and the flower thereof falleth away, but the word of the Lord endureth for ever ;" adding, in his homely and pathetic way, that the flower would again bloom, never again to fade ; that what was now sown in dishonour and weakness, would be raised in glory and power, like unto His own glorious body.   Then to my surprise and alarm, the coffin, resting on its bearers, was placed over that dark hole, and I watched with curious eye the unrolling of those neat black bunches of cords, which I have often enough seen since.   My father took the one at the head, and also another much smaller springing from the same point as his, which he had caused to be put there, and unrolling it, put it into my hand. I twisted it firmly round my fingers, and awaited the result; the burial men with their real ropes lowered the coffin, and when it rested at the bottom, it was too far down for me to see it—the grave was made very deep, as he used afterwards to tell us, that it might hold us all—my father first and abruptly let his cord drop, followed by the rest. This was too much. I now saw what was meant, and held on and fixed my fist and feet, and I believe my father had some difficulty in forcing open my small fingers; he let the little black cord drop, and I remember, in my misery and anger, seeing its open end disappearing in the gloom.

My mother's death was the second epoch in my father's life; it marked a change at once and for life; and for a man so self-reliant, so poised upon a centre of his own, it is wonderful the extent of change it made. He went home, preached her funeral sermon, every one in the church in tears, himself outwardly unmoved.* But from that time dates an entire, though always deepening, alteration in his manner of preaching, because an entire change in his way of dealing with God's Word. Not that his abiding

---

* I have been told that *once* in the course of the sermon his voice trembled, and many feared he was about to break down.

religious views and convictions were then ori-
ginated or even altered—I doubt not that from
a child he not only knew the Holy Scriptures, but
was "wise unto salvation"—but it strengthened
and clarified, quickened and gave permanent
direction to, his sense of God as revealed in His
Word. He took as it were to subsoil ploughing;
he got a new and adamantine point to the in-
strument with which he bored, and with a fresh
power—with his whole might, he sunk it right
down into the living rock, to the virgin gold.
His entire nature had got a shock, and his
blood was drawn inwards, his surface was chil-
led ; but fuel was heaped all the more on the
inner fires, and his zeal, that τι θερμὸν πρᾶγμα,
burned with a new ardour ; indeed had he not
found an outlet for his pent-up energy, his brain
must have given way, and his faculties have
either consumed themselves in wild, wasteful
splendour and combustion, or dwindled into
lethargy.*

The manse became silent; we lived and
slept and played under the shadow of that

---

* There is a story illustrative of this altered manner and matter
of preaching. He had been preaching when very young, at Gala-
shiels, and one wife said to her "neebor," "Jean, what think ye
o' the lad?" "It's maist o't tinsel wark," said Jean, neither relish-
ing nor appreciating his fine sentiments and figures. After my
mother's death, he preached in the same place, and Jean, running
to her friend, took the first word, "It's a' gowd noo."

death, and we saw, or rather felt, that he was
another father than before.   No more happy
laughter from the two in the parlour, as he was
reading Larry, the Irish postboy's letter in
Miss Edgeworth's tale, or the last Waverley
novel ; no more visitings in a cart with her,
he riding beside us on his white thoroughbred pony, to Kilbucho, or Rachan Mill, or
Kirklawhill.   He went among his people as
usual when they were ill ; he preached better
than ever—they were sometimes frightened to
think how wonderfully he preached ; but the
sunshine was over—the glad and careless look,
the joy of young life and mutual love.   He was
little with us, and, as I said, the house was still,
except when he was *mandating* his sermons for
Sabbath.   This he always did, not only *vivâ
voce*, but with as much energy and loudness as
in the pulpit ; we felt his voice was sharper,
and rang keen through the house.

What we lost, the congregation and the world
gained.   He gave himself wholly to his work.
As you have yourself said, he changed his entire
system and fashion of preaching ; from being
elegant, rhetorical, and ambitious, he became
concentrated, urgent, moving (being himself
moved), keen, searching, unswerving, authoritative to fierceness, full of the terrors of the Lord,

if he could but persuade men.   The truth of the words of God had shone out upon him with an immediateness and infinity of meaning and power, which made them, though the same words he had looked on from childhood, other and greater and deeper words.   He then left the ordinary commentators, and men who write about meanings and flutter around the circumference and corners ; he was bent on the centre, on touching with his own fingers, on seeing with his own eyes, the pearl of great price. Then it was that he began to dig into the depths, into the primary and auriferous rock of Scripture, and take nothing at another's hand : then he took up with the word "apprehend ;" he had laid hold of the truth,—there it was, with its evidence, in his hand ; and every one who knew him must remember well how, in speaking with earnestness of the meaning of a passage, he, in his ardent, hesitating way, looked into the palm of his hand as if he actually saw there the truth he was going to utter.   This word *apprehend* played a large part in his lectures, as the thing itself did in his processes of investigation, or, if I might make a word, *indagation.*   Comprehension, he said, was for few ; apprehension was for every man who had hands and a head to rule them, and an eye to direct them. Out of this arose one of his deficiencies. He *could* go largely into the generalities of a subject, and relished greatly others doing it, so that they did do it really and well; but he was averse to abstract and wide reasonings. Principles he rejoiced in : he worked with them as with his choicest weapons; they were the polished stones for his sling, against the Goliaths of presumption, error, and tyranny in thought or in polity, civil or ecclesiastical ; but he somehow divined a principle, or got at it naked and alone, rather than deduced it and brought it to a point from an immensity of particulars, and then rendered it back so as to bind them into one *cosmos.* One of my young friends now dead, who afterwards went to India, used to come and hear him in Broughton Place with me, and this word *apprehend* caught him, and as he had a great love for my father, in writing home to me, he never forgot to ask how "grand old Apprehend" was.

From this time dates my father's possession and use of the German Exegetics. After my mother's death I slept with him ; his bed was in his study, a small room,* with a very small

---

* On a low chest of drawers in this room there lay for many years my mother's parasol, by his orders—I daresay, for long, the only one in Biggar.

grate ; and I remember well his getting those fat, shapeless, spongy German books, as if one would sink in them, and be bogged in their bibulous, unsized paper ; and watching him as he impatiently cut them up, and dived into them in his rapid, eclectic way, tasting them, and dropping for my play such a lot of soft, large, curled bits from the paper-cutter, leaving the edges all shaggy. He never came to bed when I was awake, which was not to be wondered at ; but I can remember often awaking far on in the night or morning, and seeing that keen, beautiful, intense face bending over these Rosenmüllers, and Ernestis, and Storrs, and Kuinoels—the fire out, and the grey dawn peering through the window ; and when he heard me move, he would speak to me in the foolish words of endearment my mother was wont to use, and come to bed, and take me, warm as I was, into his cold bosom.

Vitringa in Jesaiam I especially remember, a noble folio. Even then, with that eagerness to communicate what he had himself found, of which you must often have been made the subject, he went and told it. He would try to make me, small man as I was, "apprehend" what he and Vitringa between them had made out, of the fifty-third chapter of his favourite prophet, the princely Isaiah.* Even then, so far as I can recal, he never took notes of what he read. He did not need this, his intellectual force and clearness were so great; he was so *totus in illo*, whatever it was, that he recorded by a secret of its own, his mind's results and victories and *memoranda*, as he went on ; he did not even mark his books, at least very seldom ; he marked his mind.

---

* His reading aloud of everything from John Gilpin to John Howe was a fine and high art, or rather gift. Henderson could not have given

> "The dinner waits, and we are tired ;"
> Says Gilpin, " So am I,"

better ; and to hear him sounding the depths and cadences of the Living Temple, " bearing on its front this doleful inscription, ' Here God once dwelt,'" was like listening to the recitative of Handel. But Isaiah was his masterpiece ; and I remember quite well his startling us all when reading at family worship " His name shall be called Wonderful, the Counsellor, the mighty God," by a peremptory, explosive sharpness, as of thunder overhead, at the words " the mighty God," similar to the rendering now given to Handel's music, and doubtless so meant by him ; and then closing with " the Prince of Peace," soft and low. No man who wishes to feel Isaiah, as well as understand him, should be ignorant of Handel's " Messiah." His prelude to " Comfort ye "—its simple theme, cheerful and infinite as the ripple of the unsearchable sea—gives a deepened meaning to the words. One of my father's great delights in his dying months was reading the lives of Handel and of Michael Angelo, then newly out. He felt that the author of " He was despised," and " He shall feed his flock," and those other wonderful airs, was a man of profound religious feeling, of which they were the utterance ; and he rejoiced over the warlike airs and choruses of " Judas Maccabæus." You have recorded his estimate of the religious nature of him of the *terribile via;* he said it was a relief to his mind to know that such a mighty genius walked humbly with his God.

He was thus every year preaching with more and more power, because with more and more knowledge and "pureness;" and, as you say, there were probably nowhere in Britain such lectures delivered at that time to such an audience, consisting of country people, sound, devout, well-read in their Bibles and in the native divinity, but quite unused to persistent, deep, critical thought.

Much of this—most of it—was entirely his own, self-originated and self-sustained, and done for its own sake,

> "All too happy in the pleasure
> Of his own exceeding treasure."

But he often said, with deep feeling, that one thing put him always on his mettle, the knowledge that "yonder in that corner, under the gallery, sat, Sabbath after Sabbath, a man who knew his Greek Testament better than I did."

This was his brother-in-law, and one of his elders, Mr. Robert Johnston, married to his sister Violet, a merchant and portioner in Biggar, a remarkable man, of whom it is difficult to say to strangers what is true, without being accused of exaggeration. A shopkeeper in that remote little town, he not only intermeddled fearlessly with all knowledge, but mastered more than many practised and University men do in

2 E

their own lines.   Mathematics, astronomy, and especially what may be called *selenology*, or the doctrine of the moon, and the higher geometry and physics ; Hebrew, Sanscrit, Greek, and Latin, to the veriest rigours of prosody and metre ; Spanish and Italian, German, French, and any odd language that came in his way ; all these he knew more or less thoroughly, and acquired them in the most leisurely, easy, cool sort of way, as if he grazed and browsed perpetually in the field of letters, rather than made formal meals, or gathered for any ulterior purpose, his fruits, his roots, and his nuts—he especially liked mental nuts—much less bought them from any one.

With all this, his knowledge of human, and especially of Biggar human nature, the ins and outs of its little secret ongoings, the entire gossip of the place, was like a woman's ; moreover, every personage great or small, heroic or comic, in Homer—whose poems he made it a matter of conscience to read once every four years—Plautus, Suetonius, Plutarch, Tacitus, and Lucian, down through Boccaccio and Don Quixote, which he knew by heart and from the living Spanish, to Joseph Andrews, the Spectator, Goldsmith and Swift, Miss Austen, Miss Edgeworth, and Miss Ferrier, Galt and Sir

Walter,—he was as familiar with, as with David Crockat the nailer, or the parish minister, the town-drummer, the mole-catcher, or the poaching weaver, who had the night before leistered a prime kipper at Rachan Mill, by the flare of a tarry wisp, or brought home his surreptitious grey hen or *maukin* from the wilds of Dunsyre or the dreary Lang Whang.*

This singular man came to the manse every Friday evening for many years, and he and my father discussed everything and everybody; —beginning with tough, strong head work— a bout at wrestling, be it Cæsar's Bridge, the Epistles of Phalaris, the import of μέν and δέ, the Catholic question, or the great roots of Christian faith; ending with the latest joke in the town, or the *West Raw*, the last effusion by Affleck, tailor and poet, the last blunder of Æsop the apothecary, and the last repartee of the village fool, with the week's Edinburgh and Glasgow news by their respective carriers; the whole little life, sad and humorous—who had been born, and who was dying or dead, married or about to be, for the past eight days.†

* With the practices of this last worthy, when carried on moderately, and for the sport's sake, he had a special sympathy.

† I believe this was the true though secret source of much of my father's knowledge of the minute personal history of every one in his region, which,—to his people, knowing his reserved manner and his

This amused, and, in the true sense, diverted
my father, and gratified his curiosity, which was
great, and his love of men, as well as for man.
He was shy, and unwilling to ask what he longed
to know, liking better to have it given him without the asking ; and no one could do this better
than " Uncle Johnston."

You may readily understand what a thorough
exercise and diversion of an intellectual and
social kind this was, for they were neither of
them men to shirk from close gripes, or trifle and
flourish with their weapons ; they laid on and
spared not.   And then my uncle had generally
some special nut of his own to crack, some thesis
to fling down and offer battle on, some " par-
ticle " to energize upon ; for though quiet and
calm, he was thoroughly combative, and enjoyed seeing his friend's blood up, and hearing
his emphatic and bright speech, and watching
his flashing eye.   Then he never spared him ;
criticised and sometimes quizzed—for he had
great humour—his style, as well as debated and
weighed his apprehendings and exegeses, shaking them heartily to test their strength.   He
was so thoroughly independent of all authority,

devotion to his studies, and his so rarely meeting them or speaking to
them except from the pulpit, or at a diet of visitation, was a perpetual
wonder, and of which he made great use in his dealings with his
afflicted or erring " members."

except that of reason and truth, and his own humour; so ready to detect what was weak, extravagant, or unfair; so full of relish for intellectual power and accuracy, and so attached to and proud of my father, and bent on his making the best of himself, that this trial was never relaxed. His firm and close-grained mind was a sort of whetstone on which my father sharpened his wits at this weekly "setting."

The very difference of their mental tempers and complexions drew them together—the one impatient, nervous, earnest, instant, swift, vehement, regardless of exertion, bent on his goal, like a thoroughbred racer, pressing to the mark; the other leisurely to slowness and provokingness, with a constitution which could stand a great deal of ease, unimpassioned, still, clear, untroubled by likings or dislikings, dwelling and working in thought and speculation and observation as ends in themselves, and as their own rewards :* the one hunting for a principle or a

---

* He was curiously destitute of all literary ambition or show; like the *cactus* in the desert, always plump, always taking in the dew of heaven, and caring little to give it out. He wrote many papers in the *Repository* and *Monitor*, an acute and clever tract on the voluntary controversy, entitled *Calm Answers to Angry Questions*, and was the author of a capital bit of literary banter—a Congratulatory Letter to the Minister of Liberton, who had come down upon my father in a pamphlet, for his sermon on "There remaineth much land

" divine method ;" the other sapping or shelling from a distance, and for his pleasure, a position, or gaining a point, or settling a rule, or verifying a problem, or getting axiomatic and proverbial.

In appearance they were as curiously unlike ; my uncle short and round to rotundity, homely and florid in feature.   I used to think Socrates must have been like him in visage as well as in much of his mind.   He was careless in his dress, his hands in his pockets as a rule, and strenuous only in smoking or in sleep; with a large, full skull, a humorous twinkle in his cold, blue eye, a soft, low voice, expressing every kind of thought in the same, sometimes plaguily *douce* tone ; a great power of quiet and telling sarcasm, large capacity of listening to and of enjoying other men's talk, however small.

My father—tall, slim, agile, quick in his movements, graceful, neat to nicety in his dress, with much in his air of what is called style, with a face almost too beautiful for a man's, had not his eyes commanded it and all who looked at it, and his close, firm mouth been ready to say

to be possessed." It is a mixture of Swift and Arbuthnot. I remember one of the flowers he culls from him he is congratulating, in which my father is characterized as one of those "shallow, sallow souls that would swallow the bait, without perceiving the cloven foot!" But a man like this never is best in a book ; he is always greater than his work.

what the fiery spirit might bid; his eyes, when at rest, expressing—more than almost any other's I ever saw—sorrow and tender love, a desire to give and to get sympathy, and a sort of gentle, deep sadness, as if that was their permanent state, and gladness their momentary act; but when awakened, full of fire, peremptory, and not to be trifled with; and his smile, and flash of gaiety and fun, something no one could forget; his hair in early life a dead black; his eyebrows of exquisite curve, narrow and intense; his voice deep when unmoved and calm; keen and sharp to piercing fierceness when vehement and roused—in the pulpit, at times a shout, at times a pathetic wail; his utterance hesitating, emphatic, explosive, powerful,—each sentence shot straight and home; his hesitation arising from his crowd of impatient ideas, and his resolute will that they should come in their order, and some of them not come at all, only the best, and his settled determination that each thought should be dressed in the very and only word which he stammered on till it came, —it was generally worth his pains and ours.

Uncle Johnston, again, flowed on like Cæsar's *Arar, incredibili lenitate*, or like linseed out of a poke. You can easily fancy the spiritual and bodily contrast of these men, and can fancy too, the kind of engagements they would have with their own proper weapons on these Friday evenings, in the old manse dining-room, my father showing uncle out into the darkness of the back-road, and uncle, doubtless, lighting his black and ruminative pipe.

If my uncle brought up nuts to crack, my father was sure to have some difficulties to consult about, or some passages to read, something that made him put his whole energy forth ; and when he did so, I never heard such reading. To hear him read the story of Joseph, or passages in David's history, and Psalms 6th, 11th, and 15th, or the 52d, 53d, 54th, 55th, 63d, 64th, and 40th chapters of Isaiah, or the Sermon on the Mount, or the Journey to Emmaus, or our Saviour's prayer in John, or Paul's speech on Mars' Hill, or the first three chapters of Hebrews and the latter part of the 11th, or Job, or the Apocalypse ; or, to pass from those divine themes—Jeremy Taylor, or George Herbert, Sir Walter Raleigh, or Milton's prose, such as the passage beginning " Come forth out of thy royal chambers, O thou Prince of all the kings of the earth !" and " Truth, indeed, came once into the world with her divine Master," or Charles Wesley's Hymns, or, most loved of all, Cowper, from the rapt "Come thou, and, added to thy many crowns," or "O that those lips had language!" to the Jackdaw, and his incomparable Letters ; or Gray's Poems, Burns's "Tam O'Shanter," or Sir Walter's "Eve of St. John,"* and "The Grey Brother."

But I beg your pardon : Time has run back with me, and fetched that blessed past, and awakened its echoes. I hear his voice ; I feel his eye ; I see his whole nature given up to what he is reading, and making its very soul speak.

Such a man then as I have sketched, or washed faintly in, as the painters say, was that person who sat in the corner under the gallery every Sabbath-day, and who knew his Greek Testament better than his minister. He is dead too, a few months ago, dying surrounded with his cherished hoard of books of all sizes, times, and tongues — tatterdemalion many ; all however drawn up in an order of his own ; all thoroughly

---

* Well do I remember when driving him from Melrose to Kelso, long ago, we came near Sandyknowe, that grim tower of Smailholm, standing erect like a warder turned to stone, defying time and change, his bursting into that noble ballad—

> " The Baron of Smaylho'me rose with day,
> He spurr'd his courser on,
> Without stop or stay, down the rocky way,
> That leads to Brotherstone ;"

and pointing out the " Watchfold height," " the eiry Beacon Hill," and " Brotherstone."

mastered and known; among them David
Hume's copy of Shaftesbury's *Characteristics*,
with his autograph, which he had picked up
at some stall.

I have said that my mother's death was the
second epoch in my father's life. I should perhaps have said the third; the first being his
mother's long illness and death, and the second
his going to Elie, and beginning the battle of
life at fifteen. There must have been something very delicate and close and exquisite in
the relation between the ailing, silent, beautiful and pensive mother, and that dark-eyed,
dark-haired, bright and silent son; a sort of
communion it is not easy to express. You can
think of him at eleven slowly writing out that
small book of promises in a distinct and minute
hand, quite as like his mature hand, as the shy,
lustrous-eyed boy was to his after self in his
manly years, and sitting by the bedside while
the rest were out and shouting, playing at hide-
and-seek round the little church, with the
winds from Benlomond or the wild uplands of
Ayrshire blowing through their hair. He played
seldom, but when he did run out, he jumped
higher and farther, and ran faster than any of
them. His peculiar beauty must have come
from his mother. He used at rare times, and

with a sort of shudder, to tell of her when a lovely girl of fifteen, having been seen by a gentleman of rank, in Cheapside, hand in hand with an evil woman, who was decoying her to ruin, on pretence of showing her the way home ; and how he stopped his carriage, and taking in the unconscious girl, drove her to her uncle's door. But you have said all this better than I can.

His time with his mother, and the necessary confinement and bodily depression caused by it, I doubt not deepened his native thoughtful turn, and his tendency to meditative melancholy, as a condition under which he viewed all things, and quickened and intensified his sense of the suffering of this world, and of the profound seriousness and mystery in the midst of which we live and die.

The second epoch was that of his leaving home with his guinea, the last he ever got from any one but himself ; and his going among utter strangers to be master of a school one half of the scholars of which were bigger and older than himself, and all rough colts—wilful and unbroken. This was his first fronting of the world. Besides supporting himself, this knit the sinews of his mind, and made him rely on himself in action as well as in thought. He sometimes, but not often, spoke of this, never lightly, though he laughed at some of his predicaments. He could not forget the rude shock. Generally those familiar revelations were at supper, on the Sabbath evening, when, his work over, he enjoyed and lingered over his meal.

From his young and slight, almost girlish look, and his refined, quiet manners, the boys of the school were inclined to annoy and bully him. He saw this, and felt it was now or never, —nothing between. So he took his line. The biggest boy, much older and stronger, was the rudest, and infected the rest. The "*wee maister*" ordered him, in that peremptory voice we all remember, to stand up and hold out his hand, being not at all sure but the big fellow might knock him down on the word. To the astonishment of the school, and to the big rebel's too, he obeyed and was punished on the instant, and to the full ; out wentthe hand, down came the "*taws*," and bit like fire. From that moment he ruled them by his eye, the *taws* vanished.

There was an incident at this time of his life which I should perhaps not tell, and yet I don't know why I shouldn't, it so perfectly illustrates his character in many ways. He had come home during the vacation of his school to Langrig, and was about to go back ; he had been renewing his intercourse with his old teacher and friend whom you mention, from whom he used to say he learned to like Shakspere, and who seems to have been a man of genuine literary tastes. He went down to bid him good-bye, and doubtless they got on their old book loves, and would be spouting their pet pieces. The old dominie said, " John, my man, if you are walking into Edinburgh, I'll convoy you a bit." " John" was too happy, so next morning they set off, keeping up a constant fire of quotation and eager talk. They got past Mid-Calder to near East, when my father insisted on his friend returning, and also on going back a bit with him; on looking at the old man, he thought he was tired, so on reaching the well-known " Kippen's Inn," he stopped and insisted on giving him some refreshment. Instead of ordering bread and cheese and a bottle of ale, he, doubtless full of Shakspere, and great upon sack and canary, ordered *a bottle of wine !* Of this you may be sure, the dominie, as he most needed it, had the greater share, and doubtless it warmed the cockles of his old heart. " John" making him finish the bottle, and drink the health of " Gentle Will," saw him off, and went in to pay the reckoning. What did he know of the price of wine! It took exactly every penny he had; I doubt not, most boys, knowing that the land-lord knew them, would have either paid a part, or asked him to score it up. This was not his way; he was too proud and shy and honest for such an expedient. By this time, what with discussing Shakspere, and witnessing his master's leisurely emptying of that bottle, and releasing the

" Dear prisoned spirits of the impassioned grape,"

he found he must run for it to Edinburgh, or rather Leith, fourteen miles; this he did, and was at the pier just in time to jump into the Elie pinnace, which was already off. He often wondered what he would have done if he had been that one moment late. You can easily pick out the qualities this story unfolds.

His nature, capable as it was of great, per-sistent, and indeed dogged labour, was, from the predominance of the nervous system in his organization, excitable, and therefore needed and relished excitement—the more intense the better. He found this in his keen political tastes, in imaginative literature, and in fiction. In the highest kind of poetry he enjoyed the sweet pain of tears; and he all his life had a steady liking, even a hunger, for a good novel. This refreshed, lightened, and diverted his mind

from the strain of his incessant exegesis.   He
used always to say that Sir Walter and Goldsmith, and even Fielding, Miss Edgeworth, Miss
Austen, and Miss Ferrier, were true benefactors
to the race, by giving such genuine, such secure
and innocent pleasure ; and he often repeated
with admiration Lord Jeffrey's words on Scott,
inscribed on his monument.   He had no turn for
gardening or for fishing or any field sports or
games : his sensitive nature recoiled from the
idea of pain, and above all, needless pain.   He
used to say the lower creation had groans
enough, and needed no more burdens ; indeed,
he was fierce to some measure of unfairness
against such of his brethren—Dr. Wardlaw, for
instance*—as resembled the apostles in fishing for other things besides men.

But the exercise and the excitement he of
most all others delighted in, was riding ; and
had he been a country gentleman and not a
clergyman, I don't think he could have resisted
fox-hunting.   With the exception of that great
genius in more than horsemanship, Andrew
Ducrow, I never saw a man sit a horse as he
did.   He seemed inspired, gay, erect, full of the
joy of life, fearless and secure.   I have heard a

* After a tight discussion between these two attached friends, Dr.
Wardlaw said, " Well, I can't answer you, but fish I must and shall."

farmer friend say if he had not been a preacher of the gospel he would have been a cavalry officer, and would have fought as he preached.

He was known all over the Upper Ward and down Tweeddale for his riding. " There goes the minister," as he rode past at a swift canter. He had generally well-bred horses, or as I would now call them, ponies ; if he had not, his sufferings from a dull, hard-mouthed, heavy-hearted and footed, plebeian horse were almost comic. On his grey mare, or his little blood bay horse, to see him setting off and indulging it and himself in some alarming gambols, and in the midst of his difficulties, partly of his own making, taking off his hat or kissing his hand to a lady, made one think of " young Harry with his beaver up." He used to tell with much fun, how, one fine summer Sabbath evening, after preaching in the open air for a collection, in some village near, and having put the money, chiefly halfpence, into his hand-kerchief, and that into his hat, he was taking a smart gallop home across the moor, happy and relieved, when three ladies—I think, the Miss Bertrams of Kersewell—came suddenly upon him ; off went the hat, down bent the head, and over him streamed the cherished collection, the ladies busy among the wild grass and heather picking it up, and he full of droll confusion and laughter.

The grey mare he had for many years. I can remember her small head and large eyes; her neat, compact body, round as a barrel; her finely flea-bitten skin, and her thoroughbred legs. I have no doubt she had Arabian blood. My father's pride in her was quite curious. Many a wild ride to and from the Presbytery at Lanark, and across flooded and shifting fords, he had on her. She was as sweet tempered and enduring, as she was swift and sure; and her powers of running were appreciated and applied in a way which he was both angry and amused to discover. You know what riding the *bruse* means. At a country wedding the young men have a race to the bridegroom's home, and he who wins, brings out a bottle and glass and drinks the young wife's health. I wish Burns had described a *bruse;* all sorts of steeds, wild, unkempt lads as well as colts, old broken-down thoroughbreds that did wonders when *soopled,* huge, grave cart horses devouring the road with their shaggy hoofs, wilful ponies, etc. You can imagine the wild hurry-skurry and fun, the comic situations and upsets over a rough road, up and down places one would be giddy to look at.

2 F

Well, the young farmers were in the habit of
coming to my father, and asking the loan of the
mare to go and see a friend, etc., etc., praising
knowingly the fine points and virtues of his dar-
ling. Having through life, with all his firmness
of nature, an abhorrence of saying " No " to
any one, the interview generally ended with,
" Well, Robert, you may have her, but take care
of her, and don't ride her fast."   In an hour or
two Robert was riding the *bruse*, and flying away
from the crowd, Grey first, and the rest nowhere,
and might be seen turning the corner of the
farm-house with the victorious bottle in his up-
lifted hand, the motley pack panting vainly up
the hill.   This went on for long, and the grey
was famous, almost notorious, all over the Upper
Ward ; sometimes if she appeared, no one
would start, and she trotted the course.   Partly
from his own personal abstraction from outward
country life, and partly from Uncle Johnston's
sense of waggery keeping him from telling
his friend of the grey's last exploit at Hartree
Mill, or her leaping over the " best man " at
Thriepland, my father was the last to hear of this
equivocal glory of " the minister's *meer*."   Indeed, it was whispered she had once won a whip
at Lanark races.   They still tell of his feats on
this fine creature, one of which he himself never

alluded to without a feeling of shame. He had
an engagement to preach somewhere beyond the
Clyde on a Sabbath evening, and his excellent
and attached friend and elder, Mr. Kello of Lind-
say-lands, accompanied him on his big plough
horse. It was to be in the open air, on the river
side. When they got to the Clyde they found
it in full flood, heavy and sudden rains at the
head of the water having brought it down in a
wild *spate*. On the opposite side were the
gathered people and the tent. Before Mr. Kello
knew where he was, there was his minister on
the mare swimming across, and carried down
in a long diagonal, the people looking on in ter-
ror. He landed, shook himself, and preached
with his usual fervour. As I have said, he
never liked to speak of this bit of hardihood,
and he never repeated it; but it was like the
man—there were the people, that was what he
would be at, and though timid for anticipated
danger as any woman, *in* it he was without fear.

One more illustration of his character in con-
nexion with his riding. On coming to Edinburgh he gave up this kind of exercise; he had
no occasion for it, and he had enough, and more
than enough of excitement in the public questions
in which he found himself involved, and in the
miscellaneous activities of a popular town mini-

ster. I was then a young doctor—it must have been about 1840—and had a patient, Mrs. James Robertson, eldest daughter of Mr. Pirie, the predecessor of Dr. Dick in what was then Shuttle Street congregation, Glasgow. She was one of my father's earliest and dearest friends, —a mother in the Burgher Israel, she and her cordial husband " given to hospitality," especially to " the Prophets." She was hopelessly ill at Juniper Green, near Edinburgh. Mr. George Stone, then living at Muirhouse, one of my father's congregation in Broughton Place, a man of equal originality and worth, and devoted to his minister, knowing my passion for riding, offered me his blood-chestnut to ride out and make my visit. My father said, " John, if you are going I would like to ride out with you ;" he wished to see his dying friend. " You ride !" said Mr. Stone, who was a very Yorkshireman in the matter of horses. " Let him try," said I. The upshot was, that Mr. Stone sent the chestnut for me, and a sedate pony— called, if I forget not, Goliath—for his minister, with all sorts of injunctions to me to keep him off the thoroughbred, and on Goliath.

My father had not been on a horse for nearly twenty years. He mounted and rode off. He soon got teased with the short, pattering steps

of Goliath, and looked wistfully up at me, and
longingly to the tall chestnut, stepping once for
Goliath's twice, like the Don striding beside San-
cho. I saw what he was after, and when past the
toll he said in a mild sort of way, "John, did you
promise *absolutely* I was not to ride your horse?"
"No, father, certainly not. Mr. Stone, I daresay,
wished me to do so, but I didn't." "Well then,
I think we'll change ; this beast shakes me."
So we changed. I remember how noble he
looked ; how at home : his white hair and his
dark eyes, his erect, easy, accustomed seat.
He soon let his eager horse slip gently away.
It was first *evasit*, he was off, Goliath and I
jogging on behind ; then *erupit*, and in a twink-
ling—*evanuit*. I saw them last flashing through
the arch under the Canal, his white hair flying.
I was uneasy, though from his riding I knew
he was as yet in command, so I put Goliath
to his best, and having passed through Slateford, I asked a stonebreaker if he saw a gentleman on a chestnut horse. " Has he white hair?"
" Yes." " And cen like a gled's ?" " Yes."
" Weel then, he's fleein' up the road like the
wund ; he'll be at Little Vantage" (about nine
miles off) " in nae time if he haud on." I never
once sighted him, but on coming into Juniper
Green there was his steaming chestnut at the

gate, neighing cheerily to Goliath. I went in,
he was at the bedside of his friend, and in the
midst of prayer ; his words as I entered were,
" When thou passest through the waters I will
be with thee, and through the rivers, they shall
not overflow thee ;" and he was not the less instant in prayer that his blood was up with his
ride.   He never again saw Mrs. Robertson, or
as she was called when they were young, Sibbie
(Sibella) Pirie. On coming out he said nothing,
but took the chestnut, mounted her, and we
came home quietly.   His heart was opened ; he
spoke of old times and old friends ; he stopped
at the exquisite view at Hailes into the valley,
and up to the Pentlands beyond, the smoke of
Kate's Mill, rising in the still and shadowy air,
and broke out into Cowper's words : Yes,

> " HE sets the bright procession on its way,
> And marshals all the order of the year ;
> And ere one flowery season fades and dies,
> Designs the blooming wonders of the next."

Then as we came slowly in, the moon shone
behind Craiglockhart hill among the old Scotch
firs ; he pulled up again, and gave me Collins'
Ode to Evening, beginning—

> " If aught of oaten stop, or pastoral song,
> May hope, chaste Eve, to soothe thy modest ear,
> Thy springs, and dying gales ;"

repeating over and over some of the lines, as

> "Thy modest ear,
> Thy springs, and dying gales."

> " —And marks o'er all
> Thy dewy fingers draw
> The gradual dusky veil."

And when she looked out on us clear and full,
" Yes—

> " The moon takes up the wondrous tale,
> And nightly to the listening earth
> Repeats the story of her birth."

As we passed through Slateford, he spoke of
Dr. Belfrage, his great-hearted friend, of his
obligations to him, and of his son, my friend,
both lying together in Colinton churchyard;
and of Dr. Dick, who was minister before him,
of the Coventrys, and of Stitchel and Sprous-
ton, of his mother, and of himself,—his doubts
of his own sincerity in religion, his sense
of sin, of God—reverting often to his dying
friend. Such a thing only occurred to me
with him once or twice all my life ; and then
when we were home, he was silent, shut up,
self-contained as before. He was himself conscious of this habit of reticence, and what may
be called *selfism*, to us his children, and la-
mented it. I remember his saying in a sort
of mournful joke, " I have a well of love, I
know it; but it is a *well*, and a *draw*-well, to

your sorrow and mine, and it seldom overflows, but," looking with that strange power of tenderness as if he put his voice and his heart into his eyes, "you may always come hither to draw ;" he used to say he might take to himself Wordsworth's lines,—

> " I am not one who much or oft delights
>   To season my fireside with personal talk."

And changing " though" into " if :"

> " A well of love it may be deep,
>   I trust it is, and never dry ;
>   What matter, though its waters sleep
>   In silence and obscurity ?"

The expression of his affection was more like the shock of a Leyden jar, than the continuous current of a galvanic circle.

There was, as I have said, a permanent chill given by my mother's death, to what may be called the outer surface of his nature, and we at home felt it much. The blood was thrown in upon the centre, and went forth in energetic and victorious work, in searching the Scriptures and saving souls ; but his social faculty never recovered that shock ; it was blighted ; he was always desiring to be alone, and at his work. A stranger who saw him for a short time, bright, animated, full of earnest and cordial talk, pleasing and being pleased, the life of the company, was apt to think how delightful he must always be,—and so he was ; but these times of bright talk were like angels' visits ; and he smiled with peculiar benignity on his retiring guest, as if blessing him not the less for leaving him to himself. I question if there ever lived a man so much in the midst of men, and in the midst of his own children,* in whom the silences, as Mr. Carlyle would say, were so predominant. Every Sabbath he spoke out of the abundance of his heart, his whole mind ; he was then communicative and frank enough : all the week, before and after, he would not unwillingly have never opened his mouth. Of many people we may say that their mouth is always open except when it is shut ; of him that his mouth was always shut except when it was opened. Every one must have been struck with the seeming inconsistency of his occasional brilliant, happy, energetic talk, and his habitual silentness—his difficulty in getting anything to say. But, as I have already said, what we lost, the world and the church gained.

When travelling he was always in high spirits and full of anecdote and fun. Indeed I knew more of his inner history in this *one* way, than during years of living with him. I recollect his

* He gave us all the education we got at Biggar.

taking me with him to Glasgow when I must have been about fourteen ; we breakfasted in "*The Ram's Horn Tavern*," and I felt a new respect for him at his commanding the waiters. He talked a great deal during our short tour, and often have I desired to recal the many things he told me of his early life, and of his own religious crises, my mother's death, his fear of his own death, and all this intermingled with the drollest stories of his boy and student life.

We went to Paisley and dined, I well remember, we two alone, and, as I thought, magnificently, in a great apartment in "*The Saracen's Head*," at the end of which was the county ballroom. We had come across from Dunoon and landed in a small boat at the *Water Neb* along with Mrs. Dr. Hall, a character Sir Walter or Galt would have made immortal. My father, with characteristic ardour took an oar, for the first time in his life, and I believe for the last, to help the old boatman on the Cart, and wishing to do something decided, missed the water, and went back head over heels to the immense enjoyment of Mrs. Hall, who said, "Less pith, and mair to the purpose, my man." She didn't let the joke die out.

Another time—it was when his second marriage was fixed on, to our great happiness and his—I had just taken my degree of M.D., and he took Isabella, William, and myself to Moffat. By a curious felicity we got into Miss Geddes' lodgings, where the village circulating library was kept, the whole of which we aver he read in ten days. I never saw him so happy, so open and full of fun, reading to us, and reciting the poetry of his youth.

His manners to ladies, and indeed to all women, was that of a courtly gentleman ; they could be romantic in their *empressement* and devotion, and I used to think Sir Philip Sydney, or Ariosto's knights and the Paladins of old, must have looked and moved as he did. He had great pleasure in the company of high-bred, refined, thoughtful women ; and he had a peculiar sympathy with the sufferings, the necessary mournfulness of women, and with all in their lot connected with the fruit of that forbidden tree— their loneliness, the sorrows of their time, and their pangs in travail, their peculiar relation to their children. I think I hear him reading the words, " Can a woman forget her sucking child, that she should not have compassion on the son of her womb ? Yea" (as if it was the next thing to impossible), " she may forget, yet will not I forget thee." Indeed, to a man who saw so little of, and said so little to his own children,

perhaps it may be *because* of all this, his sympathy for mothers under loss of children, his
real suffering for their suffering, not only
endeared him to them as their minister, their
consoler, and gave him opportunities of dropping in divine and saving truth and comfort,
when the heart was full and soft, tender,
and at his mercy, but it brought out in his
only loss of this kind, the mingled depth, tenderness, and also the peremptoriness of his
nature.

In the case of the death of little Maggie—a
child the very image of himself in face, lovely
and pensive, and yet ready for any fun, with a
keenness of affection that perilled everything
on being loved, who must cling to some one
and be clasped, made for a garden, for the
first garden, not for the rough world, the child
of his old age—this peculiar meeting of opposites was very marked. She was stricken with
sudden illness, malignant sore throat; her
mother was gone, and so she was to my father
as a flower he had the sole keeping of; and his
joy in her wild mirth, his watching her childish
moods of sadness, as if a shadow came over
her young heaven, were themselves something
to watch. Her delicate life made no struggle
with disease; it as it were declined to stay on

such conditions. She therefore sunk at once and without much pain, her soul quick and unclouded, and her little forefinger playing to the last with my father's silvery curls, her eyes trying in vain to brighten his :—

> " Thou wert a dew-drop which the morn brings forth,
>   Not fitted to be trailed along the soiling earth ;
>   But at the touch of wrong, without a strife,
>   Slips in a moment out of life."

His distress, his anguish at this stroke, was not only intense, it was in its essence permanent ; he went mourning and looking for her all his days ; but after she was dead, that resolved will compacted him in an instant. It was on a Sabbath morning she died, and he was all day at church, not many yards from where lay her little corpse alone in the house. His colleague preached in the forenoon, and in the afternoon he took his turn, saying before beginning his discourse :—" It has pleased the Father of Lights to darken one of the lights of my dwelling—had the child lived I would have remained with her, but now I have thought it right to arise and come into the house of the Lord and worship." Such violence to one part of his nature by that in it which was supreme, injured him : it was like pulling up on the instant an express train ; the whole inner organization is

minutely, though it may be invisibly hurt ; its
molecular constitution damaged by the cruel
stress and strain.   Such things are not right ;
they are a cruelty and injustice and injury from
the soul to the body, its faithful slave, and they
bring down, as in his case they too truly did,
their own certain and specific retribution.   A
man who did not feel keenly might have
preached ; a man whose whole nature was torn,
shattered, and astonished as his was, had in
a high sense *no right* so to use himself; and
when too late he opened his eyes to this.   It
was part of our old Scottish severe unsparing
character—calm to coldness outside, burning
to fierceness, tender to agony within.

I was saying how much my father enjoyed
women's company.   He liked to look on them,
and watch them, listening* to their keen, un-
connected, and unreasoning, but not unrea-
sonable talk.   Men's argument, or rather
arguing, and above all debating, he disliked.

* One day my mother, and her only sister, Agnes—married to
James Aitken of Cullands, a man before his class and his time, for
long the only Whig and Seceder laird in Peeblesshire, and with whom
my father shared the *Edinburgh Review* from its beginning—the
two sisters who were, the one to the other, as Mary was to Martha,
sat talking of their household doings ; my aunt was great upon some
things she could do; my father looked up from his book, and said,
"There is one thing, Mrs. Aitken, you cannot do—you cannot turn
the heel of a stocking;" and he was right, he had noticed her make
over this " kittle" turn to her mother.

He had no turn for it. He was not combative, much less contentious. He was, however,
warlike. Anything that he could destroy, any
falsehood or injustice, he made for, not to dis-
cuss, but to expose and kill. He could not fence
with his mind much less with his tongue, and
had no love for the exploits of a nimble dia-
lectic. He had no readiness either in thought
or word for this; his way was slowly to *think
out* a subject, to get it well "bottomed," as Locke
would say; he was not careful as to recording
the steps he took in their order, but the spirit of
his mind was logical, as must be that of all minds
who seek and find truth, for logic is nothing else
than the arithmetic of thought; having therefore *thought it out*, he proceeded to put it into
formal expression. This he did so as never
again to undo it. His mind seemed to want
the wheels by which this is done, *vestigia nulla
retrorsum*, and having stereotyped it, he was
never weary of it ; it never lost its life and fresh-
ness to him, and he delivered it as emphatically
thirty years after it had been cast, as the first
hour of its existence.

I have said he was no swordsman, but he was
a heavy shot; he fired off his ball, compact,
weighty, the *maximum* of substance in the *mini-
mum* of bulk ; he put in double charge, pointed

the muzzle, and fired, with what force and sharpness we all remember. If it hit, good; if not, all he could do was to load again, with the same ball, and in the same direction. You must come to him to be shot, at least you must stand still, for he had a want of mobility of mind in great questions. He could not stalk about the field like a sharpshooter; his was a great 68-pounder, and it was not much of a swivel. Thus it was that he rather dropped into the minds of others his authoritative assertions, and left them to breed conviction. If they gave them entrance and cherished them, they would soon find how full of primary truth they were, and how well they would serve them, as they had served him. With all this heavy artillery, somewhat slow and cumbrous, on great questions, he had no want, when he was speaking off-hand, of quick, *snell* remark, often witty and full of spirit, and often too unexpected, like lightning—flashing, smiting and gone. In Church Courts this was very marked. On small ordinary matters, a word from him would settle a long discussion. He would, after lively, easy talk with his next neighbour, set *him* up to make a speech, which was conclusive. But on great questions he must move forward his great gun with much solemnity and effort, partly from his desire to say as much of the truth at once as he could, partly from the natural concentration and rapidity of his mind in action, as distinguished from his slowness when *incubating*, or in the process of thought, —and partly from a sort of self-consciousness —I might almost call it a compound of pride and nervous diffidence—which seldom left him. He desired to say it so that it might never need to be said again or otherwise by himself, or any one else.

This strong personality, along with a prevailing love to be alone, and dwell with thoughts rather than with thinkers, pervaded his entire character. His religion was deeply personal,* not only as affecting himself, but as due to a personal God, and presented through the sacrifice and intercession of the Godman; and it was perhaps owing to his "conversation" being so habitually in heaven —his social and affectionate desires filling themselves continually from "all the fulness of God," through living faith and love—that he the less felt the need of giving and receiving human affection. I never knew any man who

---

* In his own words, "a personal Deity is the soul of Natural Religion; a personal Saviour—the real living Christ—is the soul of Revealed Religion."

2 G

lived more truly under the power, and sometimes under the shadow of the world to
come. This world had to him little reality
except as leading to the next; little interest, except as the time of probation and sentence. A child brought to him to be baptized
was in his mind, and in his words, " a young
immortal to be educated for eternity ;" a birth
was the beginning of what was never to end ;
sin—his own and that of the race—was to him,
as it must be to all men who can think, the
great mystery, as it is the main curse of time.
The idea of it—of its exceeding sinfulness—
haunted and oppressed him. He used to say
of John Foster, that this deep and intense, but
sometimes narrow and grim thinker, had, in his
study of the disease of the race, been, as it were,
fascinated by its awful spell, so as almost to
forget the remedy. This was not the case with
himself. As you know, no man held more
firmly to the objective reality of his religion—
that it was founded upon fact. It was not the
pole-star he lost sight of, or the compass he
mistrusted ; it was the sea-worthiness of the
vessel. His constitutional deficiency of hope,
his sensibility to sin, made him not unfrequently
stand in doubt of himself, of his sincerity and
safety before God, and sometimes made exist-

ence—the being obliged to continue to be—a doubtful privilege.

When oppressed with this feeling,—"the burden and the mystery of all this unintelligible world," the hurry of mankind out of this brief world into the unchangeable and endless next, —I have heard him repeat, with deep feeling, Andrew Marvell's strong lines :—

> " But at my back I always hear
> Time's wingèd chariots hurrying near ;
> And yonder all before me lie
> Deserts of vast eternity."

His living so much on books, and his strong personal attachment to men, as distinct from his adhesion to their principles and views, made him, as it were, live and commune with the dead—made him intimate, not merely with their thoughts, and the public events of their lives, but with themselves—Augustine, Milton, Luther, Melanchthon, George Herbert, Baxter, Howe, Owen, Leighton, Barrow, Bunyan, Philip and Matthew Henry, Doddridge, Defoe, Marvel, Locke, Berkeley, Halliburton, Cowper, Gray, Johnson, Gibbon, and David Hume,* Jortin, Boston, Bengel, Neander, etc., not to speak

---

* David Hume's *Treatise on Human Nature* he knew thoroughly, and read it carefully during his last illness. He used to say it not only was a miracle of intellectual and literary power for a man of twenty-eight, but contained the essence of all that was best on the philosophy of mind ; " It's all there, if you will think it out."

of the apostles, and above all, his chief
friend the author of the Epistle to the Romans,
whom he looked on as the greatest of men,
—with all these he had personal relations as
men, he cordialized with them.   He had
thought much more about them—would have
had more to say to them had they met, than
about or to any, but a very few living men.*
He delighted to possess books which any of
them might have held in their hands, and on
which they had written their names.   He had
a number of these, some very curious ; among

* This tendency was curiously seen in his love of portraits, especially
of men whose works he had and liked. He often put portraits into
his books, and he seemed to enjoy this way of realizing their authors ;
and in exhibitions of pictures he was far more taken up with what is
usually and justly the most tiresome department, the portraits, than
with all else. He was not learned in engravings, and made no at-
tempt at collecting them, so that the following list of portraits in his
rooms shows his liking for the men much more than for the art which
delineated them. Of course they by no means include all his friends
ancient and modern, but they all *were* his friends :—

Robert Hall—Dr. Carey—Melanchthon—Calvin—Pollok—Eras-
mus (very like " Uncle Ebenezer ")—John Knox—Dr. Waugh—
John Milton (three, all framed)—Dr. Dick—Dr. Hall—Luther (two)
—Dr. Heugh—Dr. Mitchell—Dr. Balmer—Dr. Henderson—Dr.
Wardlaw—Shakspere (a small oil painting which he had since ever
I remember)—Dugald Stewart—Dr. Innes—Dr. Smith, Biggar—
the two Erskines and Mr. Fisher—Dr. John Taylor of Toronto—
Dr. Chalmers—Mr. William Ellis—Rev. James Elles—J. B. Patter-
son—Vinet—Archibald M'Lean—Dr. John Erskine—Tholuck—
John Pym—Gesenius—Professor Finlayson—Richard Baxter—Dr.
Lawson—Dr. Peddie (two, and a copy of Joseph's noble bust); and
they were thus all about him for no other reason than that he liked
to look at and think of them through their countenances.

others, that wild soldier, man of fashion and wit among the Reformers, Ulric von Hütten's autograph on Erasmus' beautiful folio Greek Testament, and John Howe's (spelt How) on the first edition of Milton's Speech on Unlicensed Printing.* He began collecting books

* In a copy of Baxter's Life and Times, which he picked up at Maurice Ogle's shop in Glasgow, which had belonged to Anna, Countess of Argyll, besides her autograph, there is a most affecting and interesting note in that venerable lady's handwriting. It occurs on the page where Baxter brings a charge of want of veracity against her eldest and name-daughter, who was perverted to Popery. They are in a hand tremulous with age and feeling :—"I can say w' truth I neuer in all my lyff did hear hir ly, and what she said, if it was not trew, it was by others sugested to hir, as y' she wold embak on Wedensday. She belived she wold, bot thy took hir, alles! from me who never did sie her mor. The minester of Cuper, Mr. John Magill, did sie hir at Paris in the convent. Said she was a knowing and vertuous person, and hed retined the living principels of our relidgon, which made him say it was good to grund young persons weel in ther relidgion, as she was one it appired weel grunded."

The following is Lord Lindsay's letter, on seeing this remarkable marginal note :—

EDINBURGH, DOUGLAS' HOTEL,
26th December 1856.

MY DEAR SIR,—I owe you my sincerest thanks for your kindness in favouring me with a sight of the volume of Baxter's Life, which formerly belonged to my ancestrix, Anna Countess of Argyll. The MS. note inserted by her in it respecting her daughter is extremely interesting. I had always been under the impression that the daughter had died very shortly after her removal to France, but the contrary appears from Lady Argyll's memorandum. That memorandum throws also a pleasing light on the later life of Lady Anna, and forcibly illustrates the undying love and tenderness of the aged mother, who must have been very old when she penned it, the book having been printed as late as 1696.

I am extremely obliged to you for communicating to me this new when he was twelve, and he was collecting up to his last hours. He cared least for merely fine books, though he enjoyed, no one more so, fine type, good binding, and all the niceties of the book-fancier. What he liked were such books as were directly useful in his work, and such as he liked to live in the midst of; such, also, as illustrated any great philosophical, historical, or ecclesiastical epoch. His collection of Greek Testaments was, considering his means, of great extent and value, and he had a quite singular series of books, pamphlets, and documents, referring not merely to his own body—the Secession, with all its subdivisions and reunions—but to Nonconformity and Dissent everywhere, and, indeed, to human liberty, civil and religious in every form, for this, after the great truths, duties, and expectations of his faith, was the one master passion of his life — liberty in its greatest sense, the largest extent of individual and public spontaneity consistent with virtue and safety. He was in this as intense, persistent in his devotion, as Sydney, Locke, or old Hollis. For instance, his admiration of Lord Macaulay as a writer and a

and very interesting information.—Believe me, my dear Sir, your much obliged and faithful servant,

LINDSAY.

JOHN BROWN, Esq., M.D.

man of letters, an orator and a statesman, great as it was, was as nothing to his gratitude to him for having placed permanently on record, beyond all risk of obscuration or doubt, the doctrine of 1688—the right and power of the English people to be their own lawgivers, and to appoint their own magistrates, of whom the sovereign is the chief.

His conviction of the sole right of God to be Lord of the conscience, and his sense of his own absolute religious independence of every one but his Maker, were the two elements in building up his beliefs on all church matters ; they were twin beliefs. Hence the simplicity and thoroughness of his principles. Sitting in the centre, he commanded the circumference. But I am straying out of my parish into yours. I only add to what you have said, that the longer he lived, the more did he insist upon it being not less true and not less important, that the Church must not intermeddle with the State, than that the State must not intermeddle with the Church. He used to say, " Go down into the world, with all its complications and confusions, with this double-edged weapon, and you can cut all the composite knots of Church and State." The element of God and of eternity predominates in the re-

ligious more than in the civil affairs of men, and
thus far transcends them ; but the principle of
mutual independence is equally applicable to
each.   All that statesmen, as such, have to do
with religion, is to be themselves under its
power ; all that Christians, as such, have to do
with the State, is to be good citizens.

The fourth epoch of his personal life I would
date from his second marriage.   As I said before, no man was ever happier in his wives.
They had much alike in nature,—only one could
see the Divine wisdom of his first wife being
his first, and his second his second ; each did
best in her own place and time.   His marriage
with Miss Crum was a source of great happiness and good not only to himself, but to us
his first children.   She had been intimately
known to us for many years, and was endeared
to us long before we saw her, by her having
been, as a child and girl, a great favourite of
our own mother.   The families of my grandfather Nimmo, and of the Crums, Ewings, and
Maclaes, were very intimate.   I have heard my
father tell, that being out at Thornliebank with
my mother, he asked her to take a walk with
him to the Rouken, a romantic waterfall and
glen up the burn.   My mother thought they
might take " Miss Margaret" with them, and so

save appearances, and with Miss Crum, then a child of ten, holding my father's hand, away the three went!

So you may see that no one could be nearer to being our mother; and she was curiously ingenious, and completely successful in gaining our affection and regard. I have, as a boy, a peculiarly pleasant remembrance of her, having been at Thornliebank when about fourteen, and getting that impression of her gentle, kind, wise, calm, and happy nature—her entire loveableness—which it was our privilege to see ministering so much to my father's comfort. That fortnight in 1824 or 1825 is still to me like the memory of some happy dream; the old library, the big chair in which I huddled myself up for hours with the new Arabian Nights, and all the old-fashioned and unforgotten books I found there, the ample old garden, the wonders of machinery and skill going on in " the works," the large water-wheel going its stately rounds in the midst of its own darkness, the petrifactions I excavated in the bed of the burn, *ammonites*, etc., and brought home to my museum (!); the hospitable lady of the house, my hereditary friend, dignified, anxious and kind; and above all, her only daughter who made me a sort of pet, and was always contriving some unexpected pleasure,—all this feels to me even now like something out of a book.

My father's union with Miss Crum was not only one of the best blessings of his life,—it made him more of a blessing to others, than it is likely he would otherwise have been. By her cheerful, gracious ways, her love for society as distinguished from company, her gift of making every one happy and at ease when with her, and her tender compassion for all suffering, she in a measure won my father from himself and his books, to his own great good, and to the delight and benefit of us all. It was like sunshine and a glad sound in the house. She succeeded in what is called " drawing out" the inveterate solitary. Moreover, she encouraged and enabled him to give up a moiety of his ministerial labours, and thus to devote himself to the great work of his later years, the preparing for and giving to the press the results of his life's study of God's Word. We owe entirely to her that immense *armamentarium libertatis*, the third edition of his treatise on Civil Obedience.

One other source of great happiness to my father by this marriage was the intercourse he had with the family at Thornliebank, deepened and endeared as this was by her unexpected

and irreparable loss.   But on this I must not
enlarge, nor on that death itself, the last thing
in the world he ever feared—leaving him once
more, after a brief happiness, and when he had
still more reason to hope that he would have
"grown old with her, leaning on her faithful
bosom."   The urn was again empty—and the
only word was *vale!* he was again *viduus*,
bereft.

> " God gives us love ; something to love
>   He lends us ; but, when love is grown
> To ripeness, that on which it throve
>   Falls off, and love is left alone.
> This is the curse of time"—

But still

> " 'Tis better to have loved and lost,
>   Than never to have loved at all."

It was no easy matter to get him from home
and away from his books.   But once off, he
always enjoyed himself,—especially in his visits
to Thornliebank, Busby, Crofthead, Biggar, and
Melrose.   He was very fond of preaching on these
occasions, and his services were always peculiarly
impressive.   He spoke more slowly and with less
vehemence than in his own pulpit, and, as I
often told him, with all the more effect.   When
driving about Biggar, or in the neighbour-
hood of Langrig, he was full of the past, show-

ing how keenly, with all his outward reserve, he had observed and felt. He had a quite peculiar interest in his three flocks, keeping his eye on all their members, through long years of absence.

His love for his people and for his "body" was a special love ; and his knowledge of the Secession, through all its many divisions and unions,—his knowledge, not only of its public history, with its immense controversial and occasional literature, but of the lives and peculiarities of its ministers,—was of the most minute and curious kind. He loved all mankind, and especially such as were of "the household of faith;" and he longed for the time when, as there was one Shepherd, there would be but one sheep-fold; but he gloried in being not only a Seceder, but a Burgher; and he often said, that take them all in all, he knew no body of professing Christians in any country or in any time, worthier of all honour than that which was founded by the Four Brethren, not only as God-fearing, God-serving men, but as members of civil society ; men who on every occasion were found on the side of liberty and order, truth and justice. He used to say he believed there was hardly a Tory in the Synod, and that no one but He whose service is perfect freedom,

knew the public good done, and the public evil
averted, by the lives and the principles, and
when need was, by the votes of such men, all
of whom were in the working classes, or in the
lower half of the middle. The great Whig
leaders knew this, and could always depend on
the Seceders.

There is no worthy portrait of my father in
his prime. I believe no man was ever more
victimized in the way of being asked to
" sit ;" indeed, it was probably from so many
of them being of this kind, that the oppor-
tunity of securing a really good one was lost.
The best—the one portrait of his habitual expression—is Mr. Harvey's, done for Mr. Crum
of Busby: it was taken when he was fail-
ing, but it is an excellent likeness as well as
a noble picture ; such a picture as one would
buy without knowing anything of the subject.
So true it is, that imaginative painters, men
gifted and accustomed to render their own ideal
conceptions in form and colour, grasp and im-
press on their canvas the features of real men
more to the quick, more faithfully as to the
central qualities of the man, than professed
portrait painters.

Steell's bust is beautiful, but it is wanting
in expression. Slater's, though rude, is better.

Angus Fletcher's has much of his air, but is too much like a Grecian god. There is a miniature by Mrs. Robertson of London, belonging to my sister, Mrs. Young, which I always liked, though more like a gay, brilliant French Abbé, than the Seceder minister of Rose Street, as he then was. It gives, however, more of his exquisite brightness and spirit, the dancing light in his dark eyes, and his smile, when pleased and desiring to please, than any other. I have a drawing by Mr. Harvey, done from my father for his picture of the Minister's Visit, which I value very much, as giving the force and depth, the *momentum*, so to speak, of his serious look. He is sitting in a cottar's house, reading the Bible to an old bed-ridden woman, the farm servants gathered round to get his word.

Mungo Burton painted a good portrait which my brother William has; from his being drawn in a black neckcloth, and standing, he looks, as he sometimes did, more like a Member of Parliament than a clergyman. The print from this is good and very scarce. Of Photographs, I like D. O. Hill's best, in which he is represented as shaking hands with the (invisible) Free Church—it is full of his earnest, cordial power ; that by Tunny, from which the beautiful engraving by Lumb Stocks in this Memoir was

taken, is very like what he was about a year
and a half before his death.   All the other portraits, as far as I can remember, are worthless
and worse, missing entirely the true expression.
He was very difficult to take, partly because he
was so full of what may be called spiritual
beauty, evanescent, ever changing, and requiring
the highest kind of genius to fix it; and partly
from his own fault, for he thought it was necessary to be lively, or rather to try to be so to his
volunteering artist, and the consequence was,
his giving them, as his habitual expression, one
which was rare, and in this particular case more
made than born.

The time when I would have liked his look
to have been perpetuated, was that of all others
the least likely, or indeed possible ;—it was,
when after administering the Sacrament to
his people, and having solemnized every
one, and been himself profoundly moved by
that Divine, everlasting memorial, he left the
elders' seat and returned to the pulpit, and after
giving out the psalm, sat down wearied and
satisfied, filled with devout gratitude to his
Master—his face pale, and his dark eyes looking
out upon us all, his whole countenance radiant
and subdued.   Any likeness of him in this state,
more like that of the proto-martyr, when his

face was as that of an angel, than anything I
ever beheld, would have made one feel what it
is so impossible otherwise to convey,—the mingled sweetness, dignity, and beauty of his face.
When it was winter, and the church darkening,
and the lights at the pulpit were lighted so as
to fall upon his face and throw the rest of the
vast assemblage into deeper shadow, the effect
of his countenance was something never to
forget.

He was more a man of power than of genius in
the ordinary sense.   His imagination was not a
primary power; it was not originative, though in
a quite uncommon degree receptive, having the
capacity of realizing the imaginations of others,
and through them bodying forth the unseen.
When exalted and urged by the understanding,
and heated by the affections, it burst out with
great force, but always as servant, not master.
But if he had no one faculty that might be, to
use the loose words of common speech, original,
he was so as a whole,—such a man as stood
alone.   No one ever mistook his look, or would,
had they been blind, have mistaken his voice
or words, for those of any one else, or any one
else's for his.

His mental characteristics, if I may venture
on such ground, were clearness and vigour, in-

tensity, concentration, penetration, and per-
severance,—more of depth than width.   The
moral conditions under which he lived were the
love, the pursuit, and the practice of truth in
everything ; strength and depth, rather than
external warmth of affection ; fidelity to principles and to friends.   He used often to speak
of the moral obligation laid upon every man to
think truly, as well as to speak and act truly,
and said that much intellectual demoralization
and ruin resulted from neglecting this.   He was
absolutely tolerant of all difference of opinion,
so that it was sincere ; and this was all the more
remarkable from his being the opposite of an
indifferentist, being very strong in his own convictions, holding them keenly, even passionately,
while, from the structure of his mind, he was
somehow deficient in comprehending, much less
of sympathizing with, the opinions of men who
greatly differed from him.   This made his hom-
age to entire freedom of thought all the more
genuine and rare.   In the region of theological
thought he was scientific, systematic, and authoritative, rather than philosophical and specula-
tive.   He held so strongly that the Christian
religion was mainly a religion of facts, that he
perhaps allowed too little to its also being a
philosophy that was ready to meet out of its own

essence and its ever unfolding powers any new form of unbelief, disbelief, or misbelief, and must front itself to them as they moved up.

With devotional feeling—with everything that showed reverence and godly fear—he cordialized wherever and in whomsoever it was found,—Pagan or Christian, Romanist or Protestant, bond or free ; and while he disliked, and had indeed a positive antipathy to intellectual mysticism, he had a great knowledge of and relish for such writers as Dr. Henry More, Culverwel, Scougall, Madame Guyon, whom (besides their other qualities) I may perhaps be allowed to call affectionate mystics, and for such poets as Herbert and Vaughan, whose poetry was pious, and their piety poetic.   As I have said, he was perhaps too impatient of all obscure thinking, from not considering that on certain subjects, necessarily in their substance, and on the skirts of all subjects, obscurity and vagueness, difficulty and uncertainty, are inherent, and must therefore appear in their treatment.   Men who rejoiced in making clear things obscure, and plain things the reverse, he could not abide, and spoke with some contempt of those who were original merely from their standing on their heads, and tall from walking upon stilts. As you have truly said, his character mellowed and toned down in his later years, without in any way losing its own individuality, and its clear, vigorous, unflinching perception of and addiction to principles.

For the "heroic" old man of Haddington my father had a peculiar reverence, as indeed we all have—as well we may. He was our king, the founder of our dynasty; we dated from him, and he was "hedged" accordingly by a certain sacredness or "divinity." I well remember with what surprise and pride I found myself asked by a blacksmith's wife, in a remote hamlet among the hop gardens of Kent, if I was "the son of the Self-interpreting Bible." I possess, as an heirloom, the New Testament which my father fondly regarded as the one his grandfather, when a herd laddie, got from the Professor who heard him ask for it, and promised him it if he could read a verse; and he has in his beautiful small hand written in it what follows :—" He (John Brown of Haddington) had now acquired so much of Greek as encouraged him to hope that he might at length be prepared to reap the richest of all rewards which classical learning could confer on him, the capacity of reading in the original tongue the blessed New Testament of our Lord and Saviour. Full of this hope, he became anxious to possess a copy of the invaluable

volume.   One night, having committed the
charge of his sheep to a companion, he set out
on a midnight journey to St. Andrews, a distance of twenty-four miles.   He reached his
destination in the morning, and went to the
bookseller's shop asking for a copy of the Greek
New Testament.   The master of the shop, sur-
prised at such a request from a shepherd boy,
was disposed to make game of him.   Some of
the professors coming into the shop questioned
the lad about his employment and studies.
After hearing his tale, one of them desired the
bookseller to bring the volume.   He did so, and
drawing it down, said, ' Boy, read this, and you
shall have it for nothing.'   The boy did so, ac-
quitted himself to the admiration of his judges,
and carried off his Testament, and when the
evening arrived, was studying it in the midst
of his flock on the braes of Abernethy."—*Memoir of Rev. John Brown of Haddington*, by
Rev. J. B. Patterson.

   " There is reason to believe *this* is the New
Testament referred to.   The name on the opposite page was written on the fly-leaf.   It is
obviously the writing of a boy, and bears a re-
semblance to Mr. Brown's handwriting in mature
life.   It is imperfect, wanting a great part of
the Gospel of Matthew.   The autograph at the

end is that of his son, Thomas, when a youth at college, afterwards Rev. Dr. Thomas Brown of Dalkeith.—J. B."

I doubt not my father regarded this little worn old book, the sword of the Spirit which his ancestor so nobly won, and wore, and warred with, with not less honest veneration and pride than does his dear friend James Douglas of Cavers the Percy pennon borne away at Otterbourne. When I read, in Uncle William's admirable Life of his father, his own simple story of his early life—his loss of father and mother before he was eleven, his discovering (as true a *discovery* as Dr. Young's of the characters of the Rosetta stone, or Rawlinson's of the cuneiform letters) the Greek characters, his defence of himself against the astonishing and base charge of getting his learning from the devil (that shrewd personage would not have employed him on the Greek Testament), his eager, indomitable study, his running miles to and back again to hear a sermon after folding his sheep at noon, his keeping his family creditably on never more than £50, and for long on £40 a year, giving largely in charity, and never wanting, as he said, "lying money"—when I think of all this, I feel what a strong, independent, manly nature he must have had. We all know his saintly character, his devotion to learning, and to the work of preaching and teaching ; but he seems to have been, like most complete men, full of humour and keen wit. Some of his *snell* sayings are still remembered. A lad of an excitable temperament waited on him, and informed him he wished to be a preacher of the gospel. My great-grandfather, finding him as weak in intellect as he was strong in conceit, advised him to continue in his present vocation. The young man said, "But I wish to preach and glorify God." "My young friend, a man may glorify God making broom besoms ; stick to your trade, and glorify God by your walk and conversation."

The late Dr. Husband of Dunfermline called on him when he was preparing to set out for Gifford, and was beginning to ask him some questions as to the place grace held in the Divine economy. "Come away wi' me, and I'll expound that ; but when I'm speaking, look you after my feet." They got upon a rough bit of common, and the eager and full-minded old man was in the midst of his unfolding the Divine scheme, and his student was drinking in his words, and forgetting *his* part of the bargain. His master stumbled and fell, and getting up, somewhat sharply said, " James, the grace o' God can do much, but it canna gi'e a man common sense ;" which is as good theology as sense.

A scoffing blacksmith seeing him jogging up to a house near the smithy on his pony, which was halting, said to him, " Mr. Brown, ye're in the Scripture line the day—'the legs o' the lame are not equal.'" " So is a parable in the mouth of a fool."

On his coming to Haddington, there was one man who held out against his " call." Mr. Brown meeting him when they could not avoid each other, the non-content said, " Ye see, sir, I canna say what I dinna think, and I think ye're ower young and inexperienced for this charge." " So I think too, David, *but it would never do for you and me to gang in the face o' the hale congregation!*"

The following is a singular illustration of the prevailing dark and severe tone of the religious teaching of that time, and also of its strength :—A poor old woman, of great worth and excellent understanding, in whose conversation Mr. Brown took much pleasure, was on her death-bed. Wishing to try her faith, he said to her, " Janet, what would you say if, after all He has done for you, God should let you drop into hell ?" " E'en's (even as) he likes ;

if he does, *He'll lose mair than I'll do.*"   There
is something not less than sublime in this reply.

Than my grandfather and "Uncle Ebenezer,"
no two brothers could be more different in nature
or more united in affection. My grandfather was
a man of great natural good sense, well read
and well knowledged, easy but not indolent,
never overflowing but never empty, homely but
dignified, and fuller of love to all sentient creatures than any other human being I ever
knew. I had, when a boy of ten, two rabbits,
Oscar and Livia: why so named is a secret I
have lost ; perhaps it was an Ossianic union of
the Roman with the Gael. Oscar was a broad-
nosed, manly, rather *brusque* husband, who
used to snort when angry, and bite too ; Livia
was a thin-faced, meek, and I fear, deceitfullish
wife, who could smile, and then bite. One evening I had lifted both these worthies, by the ears
of course, and was taking them from their clover
to their beds, when my grandfather, who had
been walking out in the cool of the evening met
me. I had just kissed the two creatures, out
of mingled love to them, and pleasure at having caught them without much trouble. He
took me by the chin, and kissed me, and then
Oscar and Livia! Wonderful man, I thought,
and still think! doubtless he had seen me

in my private fondness, and wished to please me.

He was for ever doing good in his quiet yet earnest way. Not only on Sunday when he preached solid gospel sermons, full of quaint familiar expressions, such as I fear few of my readers could take up, full of solemn, affectionate appeals, full of his own simplicity and love, the Monday also found him ready with his everyday gospel. If he met a drover from Lochaber who had crossed the Campsie Hills, and was making across Carnwath Moor to the Calstane Slap, and thence into England by the droveroad, he accosted him with a friendly smile, —gave him a reasonable tract, and dropped into him some words of Divine truth. He was thus *continually* doing good. Go where he might, he had his message to every one; to a servant lass, to a poor wanderer on the bleak streets, to gentle and simple—he flowed for ever *pleno rivo*.

Uncle Ebenezer, on the other hand, flowed *per saltum*; he was always good and saintly, but he was great once a week; six days he brooded over his message, was silent, withdrawn, self-involved; on the Sabbath, that downcast, almost timid man, who shunned men, the instant he was in the pulpit, stood up a son of thunder. Such a voice! such a piercing eye! such an inevitable forefinger, held out trembling with the terrors of the Lord; such a power of asking questions and letting them fall deep into the hearts of his hearers, and then answering them himself, with an "ah, sirs!" that thrilled and quivered from him to them.

I remember his astonishing us all with a sudden burst. It was a sermon upon the apparent *plus* of evil in this world, and he had driven himself and us all to despair—so much sin, so much misery—when, taking advantage of the chapter he had read, the account of the uproar at Ephesus in the Theatre, he said, " Ah, sirs! what if some of the men who, for ' about the space of two hours,' cried out ' Great is Diana of the Ephesians,' have for the space of eighteen hundred years and more been crying day and night, ' Great and marvellous are thy works, Lord God Almighty; just and true are all thy ways, thou King of saints; who shall not fear thee, O Lord, and glorify thy name? for thou only art holy.' "

You have doubtless heard of the story of Lord Brougham going to hear him. It is very characteristic, and as I had it from Mrs. Cuninghame, who was present, I may be allowed to tell it. Brougham and Denman were on a visit

to James Stuart of Dunearn, about the time
of the Queen's trial.   They had asked Stuart
where they should go to church ; he said
he would take them to a Seceder minister at
Inverkeithing.   They went, and as Mr. Stuart
had described the saintly old man, Brougham
said he would like to be introduced to him, and
arriving before service time, Mr. Stuart called,
and left a message that some gentlemen wished
to see him.   The answer was that " Maister"
Brown saw nobody before divine worship.   He
then sent in Brougham and Denman's names.
" Mr. Brown's compliments to Mr. Stuart, and
he sees nobody before sermon," and in a few
minutes out came the stooping shy old man, and
passed them, unconscious of their presence.
They sat in the front gallery, and he preached
a faithful sermon, full of fire and of native force.
They came away greatly moved, and each wrote
to Lord Jeffrey to lose not a week in coming to
hear the greatest natural orator they had ever
heard.   Jeffrey came next Sunday, and often
after declared he never heard such words, such a
sacred, untaught gift of speech.   Nothing was
more beautiful than my father's admiration and
emotion when listening to his uncle's rapt passages, or than his childlike faith in my father's
exegetical prowess.   He used to have a list of

difficult passages ready for "my nephew," and
the moment the oracle gave a decision, the old
man asked him to repeat it, and then took a
permanent note of it, and would assuredly
preach it some day with his own proper unction
and power.   One story of him I must give ; my
father, who heard it not long before his own
death, was delighted with it, and for some days
repeated it to every one.   Uncle Ebenezer,
with all his mildness and general complaisance,
was like most of the Browns, *tenax propositi*,
firm to obstinacy.   He had established a week-
day sermon at the North Ferry, about two miles
from his own town, Inverkeithing.   It was, I
think, on the Tuesdays.   It was winter, and a
wild, drifting, and dangerous day ; his daughters
—his wife was dead—besought him not to go ;
he smiled vaguely, but continued getting into his
big-coat.   Nothing would stay him, and away
he and the pony stumbled through the dumb
and blinding snow.   He was half-way on his
journey, and had got into the sermon he was
going to preach, and was utterly insensible to
the outward storm : his pony getting its feet
balled, staggered about, and at last upset his
master and himself into the ditch at the road-
side.   The feeble, heedless, rapt old man might
have perished there, had not some carters,

bringing up whisky casks from the Ferry, seen the catastrophe, and rushed up, raising him, and *dichtin'* him, with much commiseration and blunt speech—"Puir auld man, what brocht ye here in sic a day?"   There they were, a rough crew, surrounding the saintly man, some putting on his hat, sorting and cheering him, and others knocking the balls off the pony's feet, and stuffing them with grease.   He was most polite and grateful, and one of these cordial ruffians having pierced a cask, brought him a horn of whisky, and said, " Tak that, it'll hearten ye."   He took the horn, and bowing to them, said, " Sirs, let us give thanks!" and there, by the road-side, in the drift and storm, with these wild fellows, he asked a blessing on it, and for his kind deliverers, and took a tasting of the horn.   The men cried like children.   They lifted him on his pony, one going with him, and when the rest arrived in Inverkeithing, they repeated the story to everybody, and broke down in tears whenever they came to the blessing.   " And to think o' askin' a blessin' on a tass o' whisky!" Next Presbytery day, after the ordinary business was over, he rose up—he seldom spoke— and said, " Moderator, I have something personal to myself to say.   I have often said, that real kindness belongs only to true Christians, but"—and then he told the story of these men; "but more true kindness I never experienced than from these lads. They may have had the grace of God, I don't know; but I never mean again to be so *positive* in speaking of this matter."

When he was on a missionary tour in the north, he one morning met a band of Highland shearers on their way to the harvest; he asked them to stop and hear the word of God. They said they could not, as they had their wages to work for. He offered them what they said they would lose; to this they agreed, and he paid them, and closing his eyes engaged in prayer; when he had ended, he looked up, and his congregation had vanished! His shrewd brother Thomas, to whom he complained of this faithlessness, said, "Eben, the next time ye pay folk to hear you preach, keep your eyes open, and pay them when you are done." I remember, on another occasion, in Bristo Church, with an immense audience, he had been going over the Scripture accounts of great sinners repenting and turning to God, repeating their names, from Manasseh onwards. He seemed to have closed the record, when, fixing his eyes on the end of the central passage, he called out abruptly, " I see a man !" Every one looked to that point. " I see a man of Tarsus ; and he says, 'Make mention of me !'" It must not be supposed that the discourses of " Uncle Ebenezer," with these abrupt appeals and sudden starts, were unwritten or extempore ; they were carefully composed and written out,—only these flashes of thought and passion came on him suddenly when writing, and were therefore quite natural when delivered—they came on him again.

The Rev. John Belfrage, M.D., had more power over my father's actions and his relations to the world, than any other of his friends ; over his thoughts and convictions proper, not much, —few living men had, and even among the mighty dead, he called no man master. He used to say that the three master intellects devoted to the study of divine truth since the apostles, were Augustine, Calvin, and Jonathan Edwards ; but that even they were only *primi inter pares*,—this by the bye.

On all that concerned his outward life as a public teacher, as a father, and as a member of society, he consulted Dr. Belfrage, and was swayed greatly by his judgment, as, for instance, the choice of a profession for myself, his second marriage, etc. He knew him to be his true friend, and not only wise and honest, but pre-eminently a man of affairs, *capax rerum.*

Dr. Belfrage was a great man *in posse*, if ever I saw one,—" a village Hampden." Greatness was of his essence ; nothing paltry, nothing secondary, nothing untrue. Large in body, large and handsome in face, lofty in manner to his equals or superiors ;* homely, familiar, cordial with the young and the poor,—I never met with a more truly royal nature—more native and endued to rule, guide, and benefit mankind. He was for ever scheming for the good of others, and chiefly in the way of helping them to help themselves. From a curious want of ambition —his desire for advancement was for that of his friends, not for his own, and here he was ambitious and zealous enough,—from non-concentration of his faculties in early life, and from an affection of the heart which ultimately killed him—it was too big for his body, and, under the relentless hydrostatic law, at last shattered the tabernacle it moved, like a steam-engine too powerful for the vessel it finds itself in,—his mental heart also was too big for his happiness,—from these causes, along with a love

---

* On one occasion, Mr. Hall of Kelso, an excellent but very odd man, in whom the *ego* was very strong, and who, if he had been a Spaniard, would, to adopt Coleridge's story, have taken off or touched his hat whenever he spoke of himself, met Dr. Belfrage in the lobby at the Synod, and drawing himself up as he passed, he muttered, " high and michty !" " There's a pair of us, Mr. Hall."

for gardening, which was a passion, and an inherited competency, which took away what John Hunter calls " the stimulus of necessity," you may understand how this remarkable man—instead of being a Prime Minister, a Lord Chancellor, or a Dr. Gregory, a George Stephenson, or likeliest of all, a John Howard, without some of his weaknesses, lived and died minister of the small congregation of Slateford, near Edinburgh. It is true that he was also a physician, and an energetic and successful one, and got rid of some of his love of doing good to and managing human beings in this way ; he was also an oracle in his district, to whom many had the wisdom to go to take as well as ask advice, and who was never weary of entering into the most minute details, and taking endless pains, being like Dr. Chalmers a strong believer in " the power of littles."   It would be out of place, though it would be not uninteresting, to tell how this great resident power—this strong will and authority, this capacious, clear, and beneficent intellect—dwelt in its petty sphere, like an oak in a flower-pot ; but I cannot help recalling that signal act of friendship and of power in the matter of my father's translation from Rose Street to Broughton Place, to which you have referred.

It was one of the turning-points of my father's

2 I

history. Dr. Belfrage, though seldom a speaker in the public courts of his Church, was always watchful of the interests of the people and of his friends. On the Rose Street question he had from the beginning formed a strong opinion. My father had made his statement, indicating his leaning, but leaving himself absolutely in the hands of the Synod. There was some speaking, all on one side, and for a time the Synod seemed to incline to be absolute, and refuse the call of Broughton Place. The house was everywhere crowded, and breathless with interest, my father sitting motionless, anxious, and pale, prepared to submit without a word, but retaining his own mind ; everything looked like a unanimous decision for Rose Street, when Dr. Belfrage rose up and came forward into the "passage," and with his first sentence and look, took possession of the house. He stated, with clear and simple argument, the truth and reason of the case ; and then having fixed himself there, he took up the personal interests and feelings of his friend, and putting before them what they were about to do in sending back my father, closed with a burst of indignant appeal—" I ask you now, not as Christians, I ask you as gentlemen, are you prepared to do this ?" Every one felt it was settled, and so it was. My father never forgot this great act of his friend.

This remarkable man, inferior to my father in learning, in intensity, in compactness and in power of—so to speak—*focussing* himself,—admiring his keen eloquence, his devotedness to his sacred art, rejoicing in his fame, jealous of his honour—was, by reason of his own massive understanding, his warm and great heart, and his instinctive knowledge of men, my father's most valued friend, for he knew best and most of what my father knew least; and on his death, my father said he felt himself thus far unprotected and unsafe. He died at Rothesay of hypertrophy of the heart. I had the sad privilege of being with him to the last ; and any nobler spectacle of tender, generous affection, high courage, child-like submission to the Supreme Will, and of magnanimity in its true sense, I do not again expect to see. On the morning of his death he said to me, " John, come and tell me honestly how this is to end ; tell me the last symptoms in their sequence." I knew the man, and was honest, and told him all I knew. " Is there any chance of stupor or delirium ?" " I think not. Death (to take Bichat's division) will begin at the heart itself, and you will die conscious." " I am glad of that. It was Samuel

Johnson, wasn't it, who wished not to die unconscious, that he might enter the eternal world
with his mind unclouded ; but you know, John,
that was physiological nonsense. We leave
the brain, and all this ruined body, behind ;
but I would like to be in my senses when I take
my last look of this wonderful world," looking
across the still sea towards the Argyleshire hills,
lying in the light of sunrise, " and of my friends
—of you," fixing his eyes on a faithful friend and
myself. And it was so ; in less than an hour he
was dead, sitting erect in his chair—his disease
had for weeks prevented him from lying down,
—all the dignity, simplicity, and benignity of
its master resting upon, and, as it were, supporting that " ruin," which he had left.

I cannot end this tribute to my father's friend
and mine, and my own dear and earliest friend's
father, without recording one of the most extraordinary instances of the power of will, under the
pressure of affection, I ever witnessed or heard
of. Dr. Belfrage was twice married. His second
wife was a woman of great sweetness and deli-
cacy, not only of mind, but, to his sorrow, of constitution. She died, after less than a year of
singular and unbroken happiness. There was
no portrait of her. He resolved there should
be one; and though utterly ignorant of drawing,

he determined to do it himself. No one else could have such a perfect image of her in his mind, and he resolved to realize this image. He got the materials for miniature painting, and, I think, eight prepared ivory plates. He then shut himself up from every one, and from every-thing, for fourteen days, and came out of his room, wasted and feeble, with one of the plates (the others he had used and burnt), on which was a portrait, full of subtle likeness, and drawn and coloured in a way no one could have dreamt of having had such an artist. 1 have seen it ; and though I never saw the original, I felt that it must be like, as indeed every one who knew her said it was. . I do not, as I said before, know anything more remarkable in the history of human sorrow and resolve.

I remember well that Dr. Belfrage was the first man I ever heard speak of Free-trade in religion and in education. It was during the first election after the Reform Bill, when Sir John Dalrymple, afterwards Lord Stair, was canvassing the county of Mid-Lothian. They were walking in the doctor's garden, Sir John anxious and gracious. Dr. Belfrage, like, I believe, every other minister in his body, was a thorough-going Liberal, what was then called a Whig ; but partly from his natural

sense of humour and relish of power, and partly,
I believe, for my benefit, he was putting the
Baronet through his facings with some strict-
ness, opening upon him startling views, and
ending by asking him, " Are you, Sir John,
for free trade in corn, free trade in education,
free-trade in religion ? I am." Sir John said,
" Well, doctor, I have heard of free-trade in
corn, but never in the other two." " You'll
hear of them before ten years are gone, Sir John,
or I'm mistaken."

I have said thus much of this to me memorable
man, not only because he was my father's closest
and most powerful personal friend, but because
by his word he probably changed the whole
future course of his life. Devotion to his friends
was one of the chief ends of his life, not caring
much for, and having in the affection of his
heart a warning against the perils and excitement of distinction and energetic public work,
he set himself far more strenuously than for
any selfish object, to promote the triumphs of
those whom his acquired instinct—for he knew
men as a shepherd knows his sheep, or " *Caveat
Emptor*" a horse—picked out as deserving them.
He rests in Colinton churchyard,

    " Where all that mighty heart is lying still,"—

his only child William Henry buried beside him.

But you will think I am writing more about my father's friends and myself than about him. In a certain sense we may know a man by his friends; a man chooses his friends from harmony, not from sameness, just as we would rather sing in parts than all sing the air.   One man fits into the mind of another not by meeting his points, but by dovetailing; each finds in the other what he in a double sense wants. This was true of my father's friends. Dr. Balmer was like him in much more than perhaps any,—in love of books and lonely study, in his general views of divine truth, and in their metaphysical and literary likings, but they differed deeply. Dr. Balmer was serene and just rather than subtle and profound; his was the still, translucent stream,—my father's the rapid, and it might be deep; on the one you could safely sail, the other hurried you on, and yet never were two men, during a long life of intimate intercourse, more cordial.

But I must close the list; one only and the best,—the most endeared of them all, Dr. Heugh.   He was, in mental constitution and temper, perhaps more unlike my father than any of the others I have mentioned. His was essentially a practical understanding; he was a man of action, a man for men more

than for man, the curious reverse in this of
my father. He delighted in public life, had
a native turn for affairs, for all that society
needs and demands,—clear-headed, ready, in-
trepid, adroit; with a fine temper, but keen and
honest, with an argument and a question and
a joke for every one; not disputatious, but de-
lighting in a brisk argument, fonder of wrestling than of fencing, but ready for action; not
much of a long shot, always keeping his eye on
the immediate, the possible, the attainable, but
in all this guided by genuine principle and the
finest honour and exactest truth. He excelled
in the conduct of public business, saw his way
clear, made other men see theirs, was for ever
getting the Synod out of difficulties and confusions, by some clear, tidy, conclusive " motion ;"
and then his speaking, so easy and bright
and pithy, manly and gentlemanly, grave when
it should be, never when it should not—mo-
bile, fearless, rapid, brilliant as Saladin—his
silent, pensive, impassioned and emphatic friend
was more like the lion-hearted Richard, with
his heavy mace ; he might miss, but let him
hit, and there needed no repetition. Each
admired the other ; indeed Dr. Heugh's love of
my father was quite romantic ; and though they
were opposed on several great public questions,

such as the Apocrypha controversy, the Atone-
ment question at its commencement; and
though they were both of them too keen and too
honest to mince matters or be mealy-mouthed,
they never misunderstood each other, never
had a shadow of estrangement, so that our
Paul and Barnabas, though their contentions
were sometimes sharp enough, never "departed
asunder;" indeed they loved each other the
longer the more.

Take him all in all, as a friend, as a gentleman, as a Christian, as a citizen, I never
knew a man so thoroughly delightful as Dr.
Heugh.   Others had more of this or more of
that, but there was a symmetry, a compactness, a sweetness, a true *delightfulness* about
him, I can remember in no one else.   No man,
with so much temptation to be heady and
high-minded, sarcastic, and managing, from his
overflowing wit and talent, was ever more natural, more honest, or more considerate, indeed
tender-hearted.   He was full of animal spirits
and of fun, and one of the best wits and jokers
I ever knew; and such an asker of questions,
of posers! We children had a pleasing dread
of that nimble, sharp, exact man, who made
us explain and name everything.   Of Scotch
stories he had as many original ones as would

make a second volume for Dean Ramsay. How well I remember the very corner of the room in Biggar manse, forty years ago, when from him I got the first shock and relish of humour; became conscious of mental tickling; of a word being made to carry double, and being all the lighter of it. It is an old story now, but it was new then : a big, perspiring countryman rushed into the Black Bull coach-office, and holding the door, shouted, " Are yir insides a' oot ?" This was my first tasting of the flavour of a joke.

Had Dr. Heugh, instead of being the admirable clergyman he was, devoted himself to public civil life, and gone into Parliament, he would have taken a high place as a debater, a practical statesman and patriot. He had many of the best qualities of Canning, and our own Premier, with purer and higher qualities than either. There is no one our Church should be more proud of than of this beloved and excellent man, the holiness and humility, the jealous, godly fear, in whose nature was not known fully even to his friends, till he was gone, when his private daily self-searchings and prostrations before his Master and Judge were for the first time made known. There are few characters *both sides* of which are so unsullied, so pure, and without reproach.

I am back at Biggar at the old sacramental times ; I see and hear my grandfather, or Mr. Horne of Braehead, Mr. Leckie of Peebles, Mr. Harper of Lanark, as inveterate in argument as he was warm in heart, Mr. Comrie of Penicuik, with his keen Voltaire-like face, and much of that unhappy and unique man's wit, and sense, and perfection of expression, without his darker and baser qualities.   I can hear their hearty talk, can see them coming and going between the meeting-house and the *Tent* on the side of the burn, and then the Monday dinner, and the cheerful talk, and the many clerical stories and pleasantries, and the going home on their hardy little horses, Mr. Comrie leaving his curl-papers till the next solemnity, and leaving also some joke of his own, clear and compact as a diamond, and as cutting.

I am in Rose Street on the monthly lecture, the church crammed, passages and pulpit stairs. Exact to a minute, James Chalmers—the old soldier and beadle, slim, meek, but incorruptible by proffered half-crowns from ladies who thus tried to get in before the doors opened— appears, and all the people in that long pew rise up, and he, followed by his minister, erect and engrossed, walks in along the seat, and they struggle up to the pulpit.   We all know what he is to speak of; he looks troubled even to distress ;—it is the matter of Uriah the Hittite. He gives out the opening verses of the 51st Psalm, and offering up a short and abrupt prayer, which every one takes to himself, announces his miserable and dreadful subject, *fencing* it, as it were, in a low, penetrating voice, daring any one of us to think an evil thought ; there was little need at that time of the warning,—he infused his own intense, pure spirit, into us all.

He then told the story without note or comment, only personating each actor in the tragedy with extraordinary effect, above all, the manly, loyal, simple-hearted soldier. I can recall the shudder of that multitude as of one man when he read, " And it came to pass in the morning, that David wrote a letter to Joab, and sent it by the hand of Uriah. And he wrote in the letter, saying, Set ye Uriah in the forefront of the hottest battle, and retire ye from him, that he may be smitten and die." And then, after a long and utter silence, his exclaiming, " Is this the man according to God's own heart ? Yes, it is ; we must believe that both are true." Then came Nathan. " There were two men in one city ; the one rich, and the other poor. The rich man had exceeding many flocks and herds ; but the poor man had nothing, save one little ewe lamb"—and all that exquisite, that divine fable—ending, like a thunder-clap, with " Thou art the man !"   Then came the retribution, so awfully exact and thorough,—the misery of the child's death ; that brief tragedy of the brother and sister, more terrible than anything in Æschylus, in Dante, or in Ford ; then the rebellion of Absalom, with its hideous dishonour, and his death, and the king covering his face, and crying in a loud voice, "O my son Absalom ! O Absalom ! my son ! my son !"— and David's psalm, " Have mercy upon me, O God, according to thy loving-kindness ; according unto the multitude of thy tender mercies blot blot out my transgressions,"—then closing with, " 'Yes; when lust hath conceived, it bringeth forth sin ; and sin, when it is finished, bringeth forth death.'   'Do not err,' do not stray, do not transgress, ' my beloved brethren,' for it is first ' earthly, then sensual, then devilish ;' " he shut the book, and sent us all away terrified, shaken, and humbled, like himself.

I would fain say a few words on my father's last illness, or rather on what led to it, and I wish you and others in the ministry would take to heart, as matter of immediate religious duty, much of what I am going to say. My father was

a seven months' child, and lay, I believe, for a
fortnight in black wool, undressed, doing little
but breathe and sleep, not capable of being fed.
He continued all his life slight in make, and
not robust in health, though lively, and capable
of great single efforts. His attendance upon
his mother must have saddened his body as
well as his mind, and made him willing and
able to endure, in spite of his keen and ardent
spirit, the sedentary life he in the main led.
He was always a very small eater, and nice in
his tastes, easily put off from his food by any
notion. He therefore started on the full work
of life with a finer and more delicate mechanism
than a man's ought to be, indeed, in these respects he was much liker a woman ; and being
very soon " placed," he had little travelling, and
little of that tossing about the world, which in
the transition from youth to manhood, hardens
the frame as well as supples it. Though delicate, he was almost never ill. I do not remember, till near the close of his life, his ever
being in bed a day.

From his nervous system, and his brain
predominating steadily over the rest of his
body, he was habitually excessive in his pro-
fessional work. As to quantity, as to quality, as
to manner and expression, he flung away his

life without stint every Sabbath-day, his sermons being laboriously prepared, loudly man-
dated, and at great expense of body and mind,
and then delivered with the utmost vehemence
and rapidity.   He was quite unconscious of the
state he worked himself into, and of the loud
piercing voice in which he often spoke.   This I
frequently warned him about, as being, I knew,
injurious to himself, and often painful to his
hearers, and his answer always was, that he
was utterly unaware of it; and thus it continued
to the close, and very sad it was to me who knew
the peril, and saw the coming end, to listen to
his noble, rich, persuasive, imperative appeals,
and to know that the surplus of power, if re-
tained, would, by God's blessing, retain him,
while the effect on his people would, I am
sure, not have lost, but in some respects have
gained, for much of the discourse which was
shouted and sometimes screamed at the full
pitch of his keen voice, was of a kind to be
better rendered in his deep, quiet, settled tones.
This, and the great length of his public services,
I knew he himself felt, when too late, had injured him, and many a smile he had at my
proposal to have a secret sub-congregational
string from him to me in the back seat, to be
authoritatively twitched when I knew he had

done enough ; but this string was never pulled, even in his mind.

He went on in this expensive life, sleeping very little, and always lightly, eating little, never walking except of necessity; little in company, when he would have eaten more, and been, by the power of social relish made likelier to get the full good out of his food ; never diverting his mind by any change but that of one book or subject for another ; and every time that any strong affliction came on him, as when made twice a widower, or at his daughter's death, or from such an outrage upon his entire nature and feelings, as the Libel, then his delicate machinery was shaken and damaged, not merely by the first shock, but even more by that unrelenting self-command by which he terrified his body into instant submission.   Thus it was, and thus it ever must be, if the laws of our bodily constitution, laid down by Him who knows our frame, and from whom our substance is not hid, are set at nought, knowingly or not—if knowingly, the act is so much the more spiritually bad—but if not, it is still punished with the same unerring nicety, the same commensurate meting out of the penalty, and paying " in full tale," as makes the sun to know his time, and splits an erring planet into fragments, driving it into space "with hideous ruin and combustion." It is a pitiful and a sad thing to say, but if my father had not been a prodigal in a true but very different meaning, if he had not spent his substance, the portion of goods that fell to him, the capital of life given him by God, in what we must believe to have been needless and therefore preventable excess of effort, we might have had him still with us, shining more and more, and he and they who were with him would have been spared those two years of the valley of the shadow, with its sharp and steady pain, its fallings away of life, its longing for the grave, its sleepless nights, and days of weariness and languor, the full expression of which you will find nowhere but in the Psalms and in Job.

I have said that though delicate he was never ill: this was all the worse for him, for, odd as it may seem, many a man's life is lengthened by a sharp illness ; and this in several ways. In the first place, he is laid up, out of the reach of all external mischief and exertion, he is like a ship put in dock for repairs ; time is gained. A brisk fever clarifies the entire man : if it is beaten and does not beat, it is like cleaning a chimney by setting it on fire ; it is perilous but thorough. Then the effort to throw off the disease often quickens

and purifies and corroborates the central powers
of life ; the flame burns more clearly ; there is
a cleanness, so to speak, about all the wheels
of life.   Moreover, it is a warning, and makes a
man meditate on his bed, and resolve to pull up,
and it warns his friends, and likewise if he is a
clergyman, his people, who if their minister is
always with them, never once think he can be
ever anything but as able as he is.

Such a pause, such a breathing time my
father never got during that part of his life and
labours when it would have availed most, and
he was an old man in years, before he was a
regular patient of any doctor.   He was during
life subject to sudden headaches, affecting his
memory and eyesight, and even his speech ;
these attacks were, according to the thought-
less phrase of the day, called bilious ; that is, he
was sick, and was relieved by a blue pill and smart
medicine.   Their true seat was in the brain ;
the liver suffered because the brain was ill,
and sent no nervous energy to it, or poisoned
what it did send.   The sharp racking pain in the
forehead was the cry of suffering from the an-
terior lobes, driven by their master to distraction,
and turning on him wild with weakness and fear
and anger.   It was well they did cry out ; in
some brains (large ones) they would have gone

on dumb to sudden and utter ruin, as in apo-
plexy or palsy; but he did not know, and no
one told him their true meaning, and he set
about seeking for the outward cause in some
article of food, in some recent and quite inade-
quate cause.

He used, with a sort of odd shame and
distress, to ask me why it was that he was sub-
jected to so much suffering from what he called
the lower and ignoble regions of his body; and
I used to explain to him that he had made them
suffer by long years of neglect, and that they
were now having their revenge, and in their own
way. I have often found, that the more the
nervous centres are employed in those offices of
thought and feeling the most removed from
material objects,—the more the nervous energy
of the entire nature is concentrated, engrossed,
and used up in such offices,—so much the more,
and therefore, are those organs of the body which
preside over that organic life, common to our-
selves and the lowest worm, defrauded of their
necessary nervous food,—and being in the organic
and not in the animal department, and having
no voice to tell their wants and wrongs, till they
wake up and annoy their neighbours who have
a voice, that is, who are sensitive to pain, they
may have been long ill before they come into

the sphere of consciousness. This is the true reason—along with want of purity and change of air, want of exercise,* want of shifting the work of the body—why clergymen, men of letters, and all men of intense mental application, are so liable to be affected with indigestion, constipation, lumbago, and lowness of spirits. *melancholia*—black bile. The brain may not for a long time give way, because for a time the law of exercise strengthens it ; it is fed high, gets the best of everything, of blood and nervous pabulum, and then men have a joy in the victorious work of their brain, and it has a joy of its own, too, which deludes and misleads.

All this happened to my father. He had no formal disease when he died—no structural change ; his sleep and his digestion would have been quite sufficient for life even up to the last ; the mechanism was entire, but the motive power was gone—it was expended. The silver cord was not so much loosed as relaxed. The golden bowl, the pitcher at the fountain, the wheel at the cistern, were not so much broken as emptied and stayed. The clock had run

---

* " The youth Story was in all respects healthy, and even robust ; he died of overwork, or rather, as I understand, of a two years' almost total want of exercise, which it was impossible to induce him to take."—*Arnold's Report to the Committee of Council on Education*, 1860.

down before its time, and there was no one but He who first wound it up and set it who could wind it up again ; and this He does not do, because it is his law—an express injunction from Him—that, having measured out to his creatures each his measure of life, and left him to the freedom of his own will and the regulation of his reason, He also leaves him to reap as he sows.

Thus it was that my father's illness was not a disease, but a long death ; life ebbing away, consciousness left entire, the certain issue never out of sight.   This, to a man of my father's organization—with a keen relish for life, and its highest pleasures and energies, sensitive to impatience, and then over-sensitive of his own impatience ; cut to the heart with the long watching and suffering of those he loved, who, after all, could do so little for him ; with a nervous system easily sunk, and by its strong play upon his mind darkening and saddening his most central beliefs, shaking his most solid principles, tearing and terrifying his tenderest affections ; his mind free and clear, ready for work if it had the power, eager to be in its place in the work of the world and of its Master, to have to spend two long years in this ever-descending road—here was a combination of

positive and negative suffering not to be thought
of even now, when it is all sunk under that
exceeding and eternal weight of glory.

He often spoke to me freely about his health,
went into it with the fearlessness, exactness, and
persistency of his nature ; and I never witnessed, or hope to witness, anything more
affecting than when, after it had been dawning
upon him, he apprehended the true secret of
his death. He was deeply humbled, felt that
he had done wrong to himself, to his people, to
us all, to his faithful and long-suffering Master ;
and he often said, with a dying energy lighting
up his eye, and nerving his voice and gesture,
that if it pleased God to let him again speak
in his old place, he would not only proclaim
again, and, he hoped, more simply and more
fully, the everlasting gospel to lost man, but
proclaim also the gospel of God to the body, the
religious and Christian duty and privilege of
living in obedience to the divine laws of health.
He was delighted when I read to him, and
turned to this purpose that wonderful passage
of St. Paul—"For the body is not one member,
but many. If the whole body were an eye,
where were the hearing ? if the whole were
hearing, where were the smelling ? But now
hath God set the members every one of them

in the body, as it hath pleased him. And the eye cannot say unto the hand, I have no need of thee ; nor again the head to the feet, I have no need of you. Nay, much more those members of the body, which seem to be more feeble, are necessary ;" summing it all up in words with life and death in them—"That there should be no schism in the body ; but that the members should have the same care one for another. And whether one member suffer, all the members suffer with it ; or one member be honoured, all the members rejoice with it."

The lesson from all this is, Attend to your bodies, study their structure, functions, and laws. This does not at all mean that you need be an anatomist, or go deep into physiology, or the doctrines of prevention and cure. Not only has each organism a resident doctor, placed there by Him who can thus heal all our diseases; but this doctor, if watched and waited on, informs any man or woman of ordinary sense what things to do, and what things not to do. And I would have you, who, I fear, not unfrequently sin in the same way, and all our ardent, self-sacrificing young ministers, to reflect whether, after destroying themselves and dying young, they have lost or gained. It is said that God raises up others in our place. God gives you

no title to say this.   Men—such men as I have
in my mind—are valuable to God in proportion
to the time they are here.   They are the older,
the better, the riper and richer, and more en-
riching.   Nothing will make up for this absolute loss of life.   For there is something which
every man who is a good workman is gaining
every year just because he is older, and this
nothing can replace.   Let a man remain on his
ground, say a country parish, during half a
century or more—let him be every year getting
fuller and sweeter in the knowledge of God
and man, in utterance and in power—can the
power of that man for good over all his time,
and especially towards its close, be equalled by
that of three or four young, and, it may be,
admirable men, who have been succeeding each
other's untimely death, during the same space
of time ?   It is against all spiritual, as well as
all simple arithmetic, to say so.

You have spoken of my father's prayers.
They were of two kinds : the one, formal, careful, systematic, and almost stereotyped, remarkable for fulness and compression of thought ;
sometimes too manifestly the result of study,
and sometimes not purely prayer, but more of
the nature of a devotional and even argumenta-
tive address ; the other, as in the family, short,

simple, and varied. He used to tell of his master, Dr. Lawson, reproving him, in his honest but fatherly way, as they were walking home from the Hall. My father had in his prayer the words, " that through death he might destroy him that had the power of death,— that is the devil." The old man, leaning on his favourite pupil, said, " John, my man, you need not have said ' *that is the devil;*' you might have been sure that *He* knew whom you meant." My father, in theory, held that a mixture of formal, fixed prayer, in fact, a liturgy, along with *extempore* prayer, was the right thing. As you observe, many of his passages in prayer, all who were in the habit of hearing him could anticipate such as " the enlightening, enlivening, sanctifying, and comforting influences of the good Spirit," and many others. One in especial you must remember ; it was only used on very solemn occasions, and curiously unfolds his mental peculiarities ; it closed his prayer—" And now, unto Thee, O Father, Son, and Holy Ghost, the one Jehovah and our God, we would—as is most meet —with the church on earth and the church in heaven, ascribe all honour and glory, dominion and majesty, as it was in the beginning, is now, and ever shall be, world without end. Amen."

Nothing could be liker him than the interjection, " as is most meet." Sometimes his abrupt, short statements in the Synod were very striking. On one occasion, Mr. James Morison having stated his views as to prayer very strongly, denying that a sinner *can* pray, my father, turning to the Moderator, said—" Sir, let a man feel himself to be a sinner, and, for anything the universe of creatures can do for him, hopelessly lost,—let him feel this, sir, and let him get a glimpse of the Saviour, and all the eloquence and argument of Mr. Morison will not keep that man from crying out, ' God be merciful to me, a sinner.' That, sir, is prayer—that is acceptable prayer."

There must be, I fear, now and then an apparent discrepancy between you and me, especially as to the degree of mental depression which at times overshadowed my father's nature. *You* will understand this, and I hope our readers will make allowance for it. Some of it is owing to my constitutional tendency to overstate, and much of it to my having had perhaps more frequent, and even more private, insights into this part of his life. But such inconsistency as that I speak of—the co-existence of a clear, firm faith, a habitual sense of God and of his infinite mercy, the living a life of faith, as if it was in his organic and inner life, more than in his sensational and outward—is quite compatible with that tendency to distrust himself, that bodily darkness and mournfulness, which at times came over him.   Any one who knows "what a piece of work is man;" how composite, how varying, how inconsistent human nature is, that each of us are

"Some several men, all in an hour,"

—will not need to be told to expect, or how to harmonize these differences of mood.   You see this in that wonderful man, the apostle Paul, the true typical fulness, the *humanness*, so to speak, of whose nature comes out in such expressions of opposites as these—" By honour and dishonour, by evil report and good report : as deceivers, and yet true ; as unknown, and yet well known ; as dying, and, behold, we live ; as chastened, and not killed ; as sorrowful, yet alway rejoicing; as poor, yet making many rich ; as having nothing, and yet possessing all things."

I cannot, and after your impressive and exact history of his last days, I need not say anything of the close of those long years of suffering, active and passive, and that slow ebbing of life ; the body, without help or hope, feeling its doom steadily though slowly drawing on ; the mind mourning for its suffering friend, companion, and servant, mourning also, sometimes, that it must be "unclothed," and take its flight all alone into the infinite unknown ; dying daily, not in the heat of fever, or in the insensibility or lethargy of paralytic disease, but having the mind calm and clear, and the body conscious of its own decay,—dying, as it were, in cold blood. One thing I must tell. That morning when you were obliged to leave, and when "cold obstruction's apathy" had already begun its reign—when he knew us, and that was all, and when he followed us with his dying and loving eyes, but could not speak —the end came ; and then, as through life, his will asserted itself supreme in death. With that love of order and decency which was a law of his life, he deliberately composed himself, placing his body at rest, as if setting his house in order before leaving it, and then closed his eyes and mouth, so that his last look—the look his body carried to the grave and faced dissolution in—was that of sweet, dignified self-possession.

I have made this letter much too long, and have said many things in it I never intended saying, and omitted much I had hoped to be able to say. But I must end.

Yours ever affectionately,

J. BROWN.